## "I didn't mean to convulse you."

The girl's cheery voice went on, asking, "Did you hurt yourself?"

Jim tried vainly to focus his eyes as she slid down the last foot of the embankment and stood beside him and the car. She was elf-like, dressed in what seemed to be a potato sack. Her deeply tanned oval face was screwed up in a frown.

"No, I'm not hurt," he responded vaguely, having completed his examination of her. "I do this all the time. I never did learn to park properly."

"Concussion," the girl pronounced as she thumbed back his eyelid. She smelled of lilacs and springtime. But that's nonsense, he thought. Lilacs don't bloom in the tropics. Lord, am I mixed-up. He relaxed, leaning against the car while cool water bathed his aching head....

**EMMA GOLDRICK** describes herself as a grandmother first and an author second. She was born and raised in Puerto Rico where she met her husband, a career military man from Massachusetts. His postings took them all over the world, which often led to mishaps—such as the Christmas they arrived in Germany before their furniture. Emma uses the places she's been as backgrounds for her books, but just in case she runs short of settings, this prolific author and her husband are always making new travel plans.

## Books by Emma Goldrick

### HARLEQUIN PRESENTS

### HARLEQUIN ROMANCE

Don't miss any of our special offers. Write to us at the following address for information on our newest releases.

Harlequin Reader Service
P.O. Box 1397, Buffalo, NY 14240
Canadian address: P.O. Box 603,
Fort Erie, Ont. L2A 5X3

# EMMA GOLDRICK

## love is in the cards

### *Harlequin Books*

TORONTO • NEW YORK • LONDON
AMSTERDAM • PARIS • SYDNEY • HAMBURG
STOCKHOLM • ATHENS • TOKYO • MILAN

To my sister,
Jacqui Razzano,
for her loving assistance
with the Tarot.

Harlequin Presents first edition May 1991
ISBN 0-373-11360-9

Original hardcover edition published in 1990
by Mills & Boon Limited

LOVE IS IN THE CARDS

# CHAPTER ONE

'LOOK,' the tall, thin woman snapped, 'I hired you to *follow* him.' Her jet-black hair bobbed with her anger; her stylish beauty was almost erased by the fierceness of it all.

'Yes,' Steve Shariek grumbled. He shifted his considerable overweight on to the bench opposite her in the tiny booth. 'And he went two blocks through the warehouse district and lost me completely. You wish me to do something more?' He spoke with the crisp, clipped speech of the British public school system; she had traces of New York standard in her drawl.

'I want you to find him,' Vera Helst snarled. In the dim light her doll-painted face looked grim. 'And then I want you to find out why he came here to St Vincent!'

'Yes, certainly,' the enquiry agent snapped as he looked out of the open door of Basil's Bar on to the never-ceasing sunshine on Kingstown Harbour. The ceiling of the former sugar warehouse, now converted to a bar, was high, minimising the heat of the Caribbean sun. Bamboo-slatted half-walls divided the big room, giving the illusion of privacy. Fresh and artificial flowers ran riot in the dim interior. 'So tell me again, please.'

She shook her head in disgust and sampled her rum and Coke. It had grown warm during the argument, another black mark against the man. 'His name is Marston,' she repeated slowly, as if he might be an idiot child. 'James T. Marston. Six foot three, two hundred pounds even. Long brown hair, hazel eyes. When he was eighteen his father gave him four million dollars. By the

7

time he was twenty-eight he had run it up to forty million. He's thirty-three now, and a hard man. People say he really has a heart of gold—the metal, I mean, not the spirit. Everything he touches turns a profit. A big profit. And the next time he touches something my partners and I want to share in his good luck. Now—find him!'

'Yes, well, finding him won't be too much trouble,' Steve told her. 'St Vincent is only eighteen miles long and eleven miles wide. But for finding out what he's up to—that will cost you extra.'

Sitting at a table on the other side of the bamboo wall, out of sight but not out of hearing, Jim Marston grinned and toasted the unseen pair with his glass of Perrier water. A moment later he tossed a couple of East Caribbean bills down on the bar as he strode out of the side door. Or perhaps glided would have been a better word. 'Lookit that man,' the bartender murmured to the waitress on duty. 'Look like a man, move like a tiger. Best nobody fool with that one!'

'I don' min' if I fool with 'im,' the waitress commented in her languid Island English. But by that time Marston was outside, cramming himself in behind the wheel of his rented Volkswagen van. The engine started under protest, grumbled for a moment.

He drummed his fingers on the steering-wheel as he waited for the engine to warm up. Five partners had been members of the conspiracy that drove his father to the wall. Four had been taught to regret it. The fifth, Harriman & Son, was represented by Vera Helst. A year ago he had vowed to conduct no more sting operations—but this was like manna from heaven. Dropped into his lap, so to speak, and Jim Marston was not the sort to hold his hand. So, one more sting? He smiled as the engine smoothed itself out. Smiled the way a shark smiles before he bites.

He chose the Leeward Highway. It wasn't much of a decision. One could drive up the Atlantic side on the Windward Highway, or the Caribbean side on the Leeward Highway. 'And it wouldn't make much difference,' he told the old van. If only those two in the bar, or those dozens in New York, really knew! After a month of wandering, Jim Marston had sailed his forty-foot yawl to St Vincent purely by chance, taking his first vacation in eight years. He was sick and tired of the financial rat-race, the New York establishment, the jet-set culture. More than that, the people bored him. But today his hunting instinct was aroused, and suddenly the world looked better for it.

'If I never earned another penny for the rest of my life,' he had told his mother that day a month ago, 'I could spend a million a year and not go broke until I was seventy. Why should I need more?'

'Don't ever ask me,' that saucy lady had answered. 'If your father had quit when he was your age, we might still be enjoying life. Or I might have half a dozen grandchildren to admire. How about that!'

'Hey, don't push your luck,' Jim had laughed. 'I'm going vacationing. See you after a while, lovely lady.' And off he went.

A bump in the road recalled him to attention as he wrestled to stabilise the old van. 'Road' was perhaps too dignified a name to call the two-lane track that bounced up and down like a washboard, clinging precariously to the verdant foothills as it wandered vaguely northward. 'And what would you expect,' he reminded himself, 'on an island that can hardly find enough flat space for a postage-stamp airport?'

More watchfully now, he skirted Cane Grove, climbed down and then up again out of Buccament Valley, and looked down on to the black sand of Châteaubelair Bay, all the while cognisant of the brooding green-leaf peaks to his right: Grand Bonhomme, Richmond, Mt St Andrew, and then the towering queen of them all, Mt Soufrière, whose tumult and eruptions over a thousand years or more had built this tiny island, and whose truncated cone threatened a repeat at any moment.

Consider that, he told himself glumly. The mountain manufactured the island, and one hundred thousand people live here by the mountain's bounty. And what in God's name have *you* ever done for anyone, Jim Marston? Not a thing, right? When even your own mother calls you a self-centred pirate, it just might be true! 'What do you get for a man who has everything?' that lady had said, exasperated, on his last birthday. 'A ten-ton load of humility, James!'

What do you get for a man who has everything? The thought plagued his mind just when, about ten kilometres north of Châteaubelair, he came across another little peculiarity of St Vincent. Without any warning he rounded a curve at fifty kilometres an hour, and the road came to a complete and sudden end!

The first tentative swing of the wheel alerted him. With unconscious skill he struggled to regain control as the van dropped about ten inches and began to buck and swerve towards the ditch and the post box on his right-hand side. Skill and strength held him to the path, but then something snapped in the undercarriage, and moments later he was nose down in the drainage ditch. The van coughed, choked and expired.

Jim Marston's head snapped forward, but his loosely fastened seatbelt held. Nevertheless, the shock of it all blanked him out as his chest smashed into the steering-wheel and his head bounced off its rim. Only for a moment, and then he wobbled out of the car and around to examine the damage.

'Broken axle,' a cheery female voice pronounced from just above his bent head. He looked up slowly. Rapid head movement, he had already discovered, was painful.

The Man Who Has Everything chuckled at his own position. He needed a new front axle, and had no idea what could be done about it. Feeling a little dizzy, he slid down the curve of the car's bumper and sat in the dust, still laughing.

'Oh, my, I didn't mean to convulse you,' the girl said as she left her battered grey donkey to feed on the low-level tree leaves. 'Did you hurt yourself?'

Jim tried vainly to focus his eyes as she slid down the last foot or two and stood in front of him. She was an elfin little thing, plain as a pikestaff, dressed in what seemed to be a potato sack. He blinked a couple of times to re-focus. It wasn't a potato sack. A long time ago it had had multicoloured decorations on it. It just *seemed* like a potato sack!

Her deeply tanned, oval face was screwed up into a worried frown. As for the rest of her, the dress covered everything below the neck, a huge straw hat concealed most of her head, and a pair of thong sandals made up the ensemble.

'No, I'm not hurt,' he responded vaguely, having completed his examination of her. 'I do this all the time. I never did learn to park properly.'

'Concussion,' the girl pronounced as she thumbed back his eyelid. She might have been sixteen, he assessed. Or maybe younger. He closed his eyes as she bent over him and gently stroked his cheek. She smelled of lilacs and springtime. And that's nonsense, he thought. Lilacs don't bloom in the tropics. Neither does springtime, does it? Lord, am I mixed up! He relaxed, leaning back against the car while cool water bathed his aching head.

Peggy Mitchell allowed herself one minute for dithering, and then set her practical mind to the task. His eyes were closed, but despite the half-smile on his face things weren't as good as they seemed. She thumbed back his eyelid again for a glimpse of the expanded pupil, then dipped her kerchief into the nozzle of her water-flask, and tried again. This time, as water dribbled down his shirt, he stirred.

'Hey,' he muttered, and his big eyes opened and glared balefully at her. Hazel, she thought quickly. Or perhaps green? It was hard to tell in the glare of the sun.

'I think we'd better get you into the shade,' she offered. 'Or up the hill to the house, if you think you could make it?'

'I'd sooner get to the house than sit here having a cold water bath,' he grumbled. 'Is that what you do? Sit by the road and waylay passing travellers?'

'I'm not one of the Lorelei, if that's what you mean.' There was the tinkling sound of laughter hiding behind the words as her hands kept on with the laving. 'And there's a fault in your logic. You may be a traveller, but you're certainly not *passing*. Come on, up you come.'

He managed awkwardly to get to his feet, supported by the considerable strength of her arm. As she brushed against his elbow he felt the soft strength of a full young breast. 'Not so young,' he guessed aloud as his feet balanced under him.

'What?'

'Me,' he lied. 'I mean I'm not so young as I used to be. Maybe I'd better sit down there in the shade.' Leaning on her heavily, he thumped down in the shadow of a coconut tree and settled back against its bole. Peggy settled down gracefully beside him, her full skirt flaring out around her.

'My name is Marston.' He offered a hand which she took gingerly. 'James T. Marston—Jim to my friends.'

'Mitchell,' she acknowledged. 'Peggy—to both my enemies and my friends.'

'I'm mighty lucky that you came by,' he commented. 'Heaven only knows how long I would have been sitting in that car.'

'I come down here every day at this time.' She readjusted the shape of her straw hat, and for a moment he caught the flash of ridiculously red hair. 'To meet the afternoon bus. It brings the mail, and I'm expecting—oh, dear, look what you've done to my mail box!'

Jim tried to look, but his eyes would not quite focus. 'Well, never mind,' she said with a big sigh. 'The letters can wait. What do you want to do about the car?'

'What I want to do about the car——' he started off strongly, and then changed his mind. 'It's not legal, what I want to do about the car. Whatever happened to the road?'

'That's how far they built it,' she said. 'I think it had something to do with a grant that ran out—or something like that. Anyway, that's where it stops. We have a number of accidents there; oh, maybe two or three a year.'

'Wow,' he chuckled. The laughter moved his head and he winced. 'Two or three a year? Sounds like a terrible traffic problem! So tell me, what are my options with the car?'

She smiled at him for the first time. Her oval little face dimpled on both sides of her mouth, and her teeth sparkled at him. There was a gleam in her eyes too. Green eyes. Carefully Jim Vincent began to reassess his benefactor. About five feet four, with a face transformed into beauty when she smiled. Half-hidden red hair that seemed almost flame-like. And, hidden behind that sack of a dress, breasts that would startle a caring man. And heaven knows what else is hidden, he reasoned.

'I don't like that,' she said quietly but firmly.

'Don't like what?' He was beginning to feel better, more sure of himself.

'I don't like you looking me up and down as if I were a side of beef,' she stated flatly. 'Now, about your car. Henry has a team of oxen. He could tow the car to his forge and fix the axle.' She came up to her knees as if waiting for something, her eyes on the road, but the moment passed and she settled back on her heels. 'I forgot to tell you. Henry is our blacksmith, among other things. He can fix anything.'

'It's only a rental,' Jim returned. 'I'm not sure what——'

'He could tow it back to Kingstown,' she interjected with a smile. 'Henry would like that. It's an all-day job, of course. He'd have to charge pretty heavily—say, oh, five dollars?'

She was watching his face for the blink—when it failed to come she almost doubled the price. 'American, of course,' she added.

'OK,' he chuckled. 'I agree. Before anything else is added on. Have Henry tow it back to Kingstown. For five dollars, right?'

'American,' she insisted. He didn't seem disturbed by it at all. On an island where fifty per cent were unemployed, and five dollars (East Caribbean) was a full week's wage, he didn't seem to care. 'Now, why don't we get you up to the house?' She waved vaguely up the mountain.

'I—don't think I could climb very far,' he protested as she pulled him back to his feet.

'I'll walk, you ride,' she said quietly. 'Satan here will be glad to bear you.' But when she strolled over to where the little grey donkey was still grazing, Satan seemed to have all sorts of objections. It wasn't until Peggy seized his bridle and gave his head a good shake that the donkey condescended to walk over to the coconut tree.

'I—get to ride that thing?' He had managed to get to his feet, still leaning against the bole of the tree. His mind was fuzzy, and every time he moved the world seemed to run in circles.

'Of course,' Peggy said cheerfully. 'You just sit down here, and——' she patted the spiny backbone just forward of the stubby tail.

'Hey,' he protested, moving out into the sun to join them. 'The beast doesn't look big enough to——'

'He's very strong,' she insisted firmly.

'And I'd have to spend the whole trip trying to hold my legs up off the ground!' The donkey brayed and kicked a couple of times.

'Now you've done it,' she sighed. 'You insulted him. Now he won't let either one of us ride! I wish you hadn't done that!'

'Yeah, I wish I hadn't either,' he grumbled. 'Lead on, Annie Oakley!'

'Who?'

'I beg your pardon. Lead on, Miss—Mitchell, was it?'

'Yes, it was. And it still is,' she sighed as she patted the donkey on his hindquarters and watched as the little beast finally agreed to accept the burden.

That's a danger signal, if I've ever heard one, he thought as he awkwardly swung his leg over the donkey's back. She wants badly to change her name from Mitchell to—what, almost anything else? She's too young to be husband-hunting, and I'm too old to play the wedding game! Nevertheless, he found it fascinating to watch her gracefully scramble along ahead of him, her hips swaying so that even the potato sack was attractive!

It was her third trip up the mountain that day, and Peggy was tired. She hadn't slept well for the past six months, not since the day Mama died. The week before Papa ran off. One more frustrating day. No letters at all—well, perhaps there might be something under the wreckage after Henry had towed the car away. But it had been more than three weeks since her brother Andrew had written. And more than six months since the letter had gone out to Chicago, to Simon & Poke, her grandfather's lawyers. A long time to wait for notice about her mother's inheritance, if any. Perhaps it never would come. And this poor soul with the knock on his noggin! Just because he can move his arms and legs he thinks he's healed. Poor man. Poor, handsome man!

When they came up over the edge of the cliff-path on to the little plateau where the house stood she took a deep breath. She always did, at this point. Located some four hundred feet above sea level, with a view outward on to the placid Caribbean, the old farmhouse gave her the sense of security she needed after following her father over half the Caribbean.

It was a typical tropical mountain home, of a single storey, but built up and down the indentations of the plateau so that it looked as if the builders had lost their way. Concrete pilings supported it above the ground, both to keep the floors cool, and to lessen the invasion of neighbourhood crawlies. A wide-screened veranda surrounded the whole construction. Flowers stood in proud masses in every corner. A dog, out in the kennels at the back, barked a solitary welcome. The noise brought an ancient black woman to the door.

'Who be this man?' The soft, mixed dialect was entirely different from the clipped tones of the centre of the city. It had a gentle welcoming sound to it.

'There was an accident,' Peggy answered. 'He's a sort of——'

'Bum? Why you always pick up the derelicts, baby?'

'He's not exactly a derelict,' Peggy muttered as she guided him up the six steps that led to the door. Sighed because she wasn't exactly sure what he *was*. 'His car went off the road and gave him a bang on his head. Help me get him to the couch, Bea.'

Bea, who was an inch shorter than Peggy, slid his other arm over her shoulder and accepted some of his weight. 'I'm really not all that damaged,' he told them both, but went willingly, and felt considerable relief when the soft cushions of the couch rose around him.

'There now. You get he feet up, missy, while Bea go find him something for that head.'

Peggy's laughing smile flashed as she struggled with him. He had a great deal of leg, this 'derelict'. They were knobbly suntanned extremities showing below his shorts. And he had heavy shoulder muscles, also well-tanned, gleaming through the V-neck of his sports shirt, as well as a craggy but handsome face, and those eyes, which were open and laughing at her now!

'You needn't laugh,' she complained as she unlaced his shoes.

'I'm not laughing,' he chuckled. 'I wouldn't *dare* laugh. It just struck me that it's been years since I received all this personalised attention.'

'You hate it?' Finished with his shoes, Peg flipped her straw hat off on to the adjacent chair and ran her hands through her hair. She heard him draw his breath in sharply, but missed the amazement that shadowed his face. Her brilliant auburn hair, sparkling in the intermittent shadows of the room, clung tightly to her scalp in a riot of tight natural curls. Almost unconsciously she ran her fingers through it to restore some order. The curls parted for a moment, and then sprang back exactly to where they had been before she bothered.

'No, I don't hate it,' he admitted. 'Any man can stand a little pampering now and then, you know.'

'No, I'm afraid I don't know,' she replied gently. 'I don't have a great deal of—don't wiggle your head like that!'

'It feels as if it might come off,' he groaned. 'What——'

'The pupils of your eyes are dilated. You probably have concussion. Just stretch out there and relax. It might go away in an hour or two—or a day or two. Whichever.'

Despite his dizziness he grinned. 'Yeah. Whichever. And if it doesn't?'

'Then perhaps it will go away in a week or two,' she said firmly. 'Now, I have to go and change. You lie there and be quiet.'

'Yes, ma'am,' he answered. Peg got up from the couch and smoothed down her dress. He had answered that flippantly, as if taking orders was something he seldom did. She hesitated for a second, and then dashed down the hall for her own bedroom.

Her mirror had been her mother's, and was stained in rose to reflect gently on the ladies. But it told no lies about Peggy. She grimaced at herself as she quickly removed the dress. It wasn't much to look at, but it was calf-length, and highly suitable for donkey-riding—especially a donkey like Satan, who hadn't been named for his good humour! Under the dress she wore nothing but a pair of briefs. And still the mirror didn't lie.

Too thin, she told herself, with the bones of her shoulders almost out of the flesh. Her ribcage showed bone too as she took a deep breath, elevating her too-large breasts into disgusting prominence. Only her flat stomach and her gently curving hips met with her satisfaction. And her legs. Long for the height of her, well-shaped. Sexy, she told herself, and then laughed. The word had a devilish sound to it, but Bea had never approved of the term.

Selection of a new dress wasn't difficult; there wasn't a large number of them hanging in her wardrobe. But the blue cotton was her favourite. It fitted loosely, allowing maximum air circulation, and yet managed to hug her here and there as she moved. Mostly there, she teased herself sarcastically as she looked back over her shoulder and patted one nicely curved buttock. It took but another moment to brush her hair again. Long hair it had been not more than three months ago, but the strain of the house, and the Co-operative's needs had shown her the wisdom of cutting it short. An altogether more adult woman walked slowly down the hall, balancing inexpertly on her two-inch heels. Bea was there before her, and the man was sitting up.

'He comes from New York,' the old woman announced, in tones that indicated it was only accessible through the Mars Space Port.

'Where's your daughter?' Jim Marston interrupted. He was feeling decidedly queasy, hardly able to hold his head up, and his chest was aching.

'Daughter?' Peg detoured around the couch and stopped by Bea's chair. 'New York? I had a grandfather who lived near New York. In Chicago. His name was Patrick Brennan. I don't suppose you knew him, Mr Marston?'

'Can't say that I do. Although Chicago is pretty close to New York.' He grinned, an earsplitting thing that took ten years off his age. 'I suppose there might be fifty thousand Brennans in New York. Are you the same little girl that met me at the road's end, or are you her mother?'

'The very one,' Peg said solemnly, and then giggled. 'It's true, isn't it. Clothes make the woman? I'm afraid I'm not very good at mainland geography. Are you saying that New York and Chicago are *not* next-door neighbours? That comes of a haphazard education. As Munoz Marin said, I grew up to be illiterate in two languages. Are you feeling better?'

'Yes. Your—Bea—gave me some medicine.'

'Give him a glass of herbal tea, is what I did,' Bea chimed in. 'Clothes make the man, too. Now could I know how many we are for supper?'

'Well, of course Mr Marston is staying,' Peggy blurted out, turning red as she did so.

'Jim,' he insisted. 'Call me Jim. And perhaps I'd better get back to Kingstown?'

'Not with that cracked head,' Bea said firmly. 'I gonna get the first-aid kit.'

'And, besides, there's no bus until tomorrow noon, and you'd have to walk all the way back to Châteaubelair—or else ride my donkey to——'

'I'll stay,' he interrupted, groaning. 'I'll stay. I'll promise you anything rather than ride that burro another step!'

'Donkey,' Bea corrected. 'Donkey. We don't have burros on St Vincent. On this island we speak the French and the English. No Spanish, you comprehend.' It was her exit cue, and she took it, stopping only long enough to display a full set of marvellous teeth, the gift of a diet containing a great deal of fish.

'Well, now,' Peggy said, as she sat down opposite him in what had been her father's favourite chair. 'Let's have a look at you.' It was hard not to blush. Her thoughts were running away with her. Strange thoughts, that caused her heart to pound a little faster, and sent a drop of perspiration running down her neck into the declivity between her breasts.

'Yes, that's a good start,' he said softly. She could feel the weight of his words running over her, fingering her, tasting her. And then his eyes closed, and he leaned back against the pillow.

She shrugged off the feeling and stood up to take the basin of water Bea had brought. 'Now stop squirming,' she commanded as she gently swabbed at the knot growing on his forehead. 'Have we any ice left, Bea?'

'Got about enough to put in a whisky soda,' Bea replied. 'We put it on he head, it don't do much good.'

'I'd rather have it in my stomach,' he grumbled, opening one eye. 'Surrounded by the whisky.'

'Fat chance,' she murmured as she bent over for a closer examination. 'People with concussions don't need a shot of alcohol on top of it. Hey, let me go!'

His hands had snatched at her, pulling her down a little closer, pressing her full breasts flat against his chest. She began to work her way loose. He was a big man, but not very strong at the moment. And after a blow to the head, men often had these little delusions about being Tarzan, or some such. And besides, it hadn't been all that terrible. There was a nice feeling about him, a purely masculine smell that was delightful.

'Not so little,' he continued softly, and then seemed to catch himself, like a cat which has worried a trapped mouse, and now offered it a chance to escape.

'I have this headache,' he continued. 'Haven't had a headache in twenty years. Thought you were a little thing, but you're not, are you?'

'Perhaps not too big,' she agreed placidly. 'But I think we'd better get you to bed, Mr Marston.'

He managed to pry one eye open again. 'Oh? Are you the local doctor?'

'No, but I am the local nurse, and that's all you'll find in these parts.' Despite his dazed condition he could hear the crack of authority. It brought a weak grin as he allowed the pair of them to walk him down the hall and into a bedroom. At which point everything went black for James T. Marston.

He awoke to the smell of coffee, the brilliance of morning, a subdued susurrus of conversation in the next room, and the knowledge that someone had stripped him naked under his sheet. It took more than a moment to remember where he was, but as it came back he smiled. The prospect of a new sting operation, the road that ran out, the mean little donkey, the buried post box, and the woman! He had to stop thinking of her as a girl; she wasn't. And his head! He moved it slightly, and regretted. The groan brought instant attention.

Peggy Mitchell was first through the door. Dressed in work clothes this morning, he noticed. Dungarees, a navy blue blouse, her hair tied back out of the way. And two aspirins in her outstretched hand. 'Take these.'

It didn't seem worth an argument. Stretched out flat on *her* bed he could hardly roar that Jim Marston didn't take orders, he gave them! Swallowing was a little difficult. He put his mind to it and succeeded.

'I really ought to contact my headquarters,' he murmured. 'Might I use your phone?'

'Telephone?'

'Stupid of me, isn't it,' he said weakly. 'No telephone?'

'There's one down at the farm in Buccament Valley,' she offered tentatively, 'but that's quite a walk from here.' And then her anger overcame her caution. He had no right to criticise the way they lived. 'And we don't have electricity, either,' she snapped. 'But we do have running water!'

'Hey, I'm sorry. I didn't mean to criticise.'

She was instantly mollified. 'It's my turn to apologise,' she said. 'Look, we're having our weekly planning meeting. If you'll excuse me for a moment until all the orders are straight, we'll have a talk. And I'll ask Bea to fix you a little something for breakfast.'

Before he could phrase a question she was gone, but in no more than ten minutes was back again, her cool hands fussing with his pillow, propping him up a little. When Bea brought in the coffee he sipped in appreciation, and felt so much better that his curiosity began to break through.

'Orders for the week?'

'T'aint right,' Bea interjected. 'Slip of a girl like you running the whole plantation!'

'Bea!' The black woman was still muttering as she walked out of the room. 'Bea will never get over it,' Peg sighed, as she pulled up a chair beside the bed and picked up his hand.

His hunting instincts rang an alarm in his battered head, until he realised that she was counting his pulserate. 'You're a trained nurse?'

'Yes. Trained in Santurce,' she replied as she made notes on a little card. 'In Puerto Rico, that is. Well, my mother was ill for years. It seemed best for us to have our own nurse in the family. And then Dad had this chance on St Vincent—a bargain sale, you might say.'

'You don't sound as if it were?'

'At the time it *sounded* too good to be true.' She ran her hand gently through his hair, and started to unbutton his shirt. Once again his alarm bells went off. A bachelor millionaire was, he knew, a contradiction in terms! But once again her light, cool hands explored the bruises on his chest, and then covered him up again. 'I don't think you have any broken ribs,' she reported, and then continued.

'Yes, it all sounded like a bargain, and Dad sold everything we had and bought two hundred and eighty-eight acres down here. Well, he and the bank, you understand.'

'A heavy mortgage? Yes, I understand. But what was the problem?'

'You'll see when you get up. Tomorrow, or the day after,' she told him. He started to protest, and stopped again. 'All you need to do is look out of the window,' she continued. 'We're on the west flank of Mt Soufrière. In 1979 it erupted. Not a great volcanic action, but it ruined all the crops, and the original owners were too frightened to stay on! I'm sure we could have got it for half the price, but my dad was never a good businessman.'

'And so now you're running the whole farm?'

'Only temporarily.' Her busy hands straightened out his sheets. 'My brother Andrew is Stateside, studying agriculture at the University of Massachusetts. When he comes back he'll take over.' She said it all so casually that for a moment he was fooled. But then, a slip of a girl running a two-hundred-and-eighty-eight-acre plantation, he thought? Bea's right. Her brother ought to be right here working! Or——

'Ah. Your mother died recently?'

'Six months ago. She had been ill for so long——'

'And you miss her?'

'Yes, of course,' Peggy sighed. 'But—I'm not grieving. I did all that during all the months she was sick. She was in such pain for so long, it was almost as if—the final day was a blessing to her and to us. And if we really believe what the Church teaches, she is surely in a better place now?'

'Of course,' he muttered, not sure of any such thing. It had been so long since he had gone to church, or even thought about its teachings, that he had to grope for something to say.

'And your father?'

Her head snapped up, and he could see the blaze in her eyes. 'My father was—not a strong man,' she said coldly. 'He—went away. Just after Mother died.' Jim Marston might know little about religion, but he had made his fortune on his judgement of people. The girl before him mourned more for the father she had misjudged, the man who 'went away', than for her mother, who had died in the comfort of her faith.

'So that leaves you all alone?'

'Not exactly. There's Bea, and there's——'

'And this man you were expecting to meet?'

She had taken a tissue from the box on the table beside her, and was twisting it up into tortured shapes between her long, thin fingers. 'It was just a letter I was expecting, not a man,' she said, and the incipient tear was cut off as she sniffed and took control again. 'From the lawyers. Simon & Poke, Chicago. Mother said that Grandfather— that he would help us if he just knew, and she sent him a letter just before she died. So I thought—you're not a lawyer, are you?'

'Me? Not at all.' The laugh that followed displayed his appreciation of lawyers, just below cannibals, and slightly above used-car salesmen. It fitted in well with Peggy's own assessment.

But Jim Marston had come a cropper himself in the affair of his own father, and knew the pain that could be associated with it all. 'Look,' he said, 'maybe I could help. A little advice, something like that?'

The grin was back on her face again. 'Somehow, Mr Marston——'

'Jim,' he interrupted.

'OK, Jim. Somehow I don't see you as being too much help around a farm. Especially not today, and probably not tomorrow. And right now, since someone has to slop the pigs, and someone has to post the books and pay the bills—and I'm that someone in both cases—why don't you lie back there against the pillow, while Bea makes you a real breakfast?'

It was hard not to respond to that grin. He smiled back at her, determined to ignore the itch that was niggling in the back of his mind. No one likes to be done good to, his conscience nagged. But maybe I can kill two birds with one stone, he argued back. It was a dilemma. When she straightened his sheets one last time he watched her walk out of the room, to be replaced by Bea, bearing a full tray.

The little old lady bustled around the bed, re-smoothing the sheets, elevating his head, setting the tray across his lap. And then she stood there glaring at him.

'Did I do something wrong?' he asked.

'I don' know,' the housekeeper replied. 'I ain't worried about what you done, man, I worries about what you gonna do. An' I gonna tell you—it ain't gonna be nothin' to do with my baby! Miss Peggy, she one good girl. She know plenty people, my girl, but she don' know from nothin' about men like you. So you listen up, Mr James Marston, if that's your real name. You keeps you hands in you pockets around here, or they gonna be cut off at the elbows. You hear me?'

'I do believe I do,' he murmured. The eggs tasted far better than the lecture, the coffee refill was even better than the first cup. And I can afford the finger-shaking as long as the food is this good, he told himself. So he ventured a tentative smile, in exchange for another glare, and finished his breakfast. As he dropped off in another nap, a smiling face haunted him, an oval, well-tanned face, surrounded with a myriad auburn curls. He slept through the remainder of the day, and on into the dawning of the next.

# CHAPTER TWO

SUNRISE was a peculiar time on a tropical island. People often tended to think of it as a spectacle, a time when Sol heralded his coming and then vaulted over the horizon into the sky in a blaze of glory. Of course, it happened like that—on the eastward side of islands. But on the westward side of a range of towering mountains it became something else entirely.

The day would begin with a paling of the darkness, a gradual increase of light, and not until the sun inched its way over the mountains about eight o'clock would the real day begin. Not that the people objected, Peggy told herself whimsically as she finished with the pigs. Most of St Vincent's citizens were not afflicted with the terrible Calvinist work ethic, and would not object to a few more hours of sleep-time. It was the third day of the coming—of Jim Marston's coming, that was—and she still found him rattling around inside her head. Only hard physical labour seemed to force his picture out of her mind! So she raked out the barn, turned the goats loose to fend for themselves, straightened to stretch her creaking back, and went off to the house for a wash and breakfast.

'Bea? Bea, I'm finished outside!'

'For the moment, you mean,' the housekeeper muttered. 'Little slip of a girl like you, doin' field work! Wash you hands again! Don' know when I seen a terribler time!'

'Terribler?' Peg chuckled as she went over to the kitchen sink and scrubbed her hands one more time.

'Don't mock an ole lady,' Bea grumbled. 'People makes the words; the words don't make peoples! We got oatmeal. What you want for breakfast?'

'Well, considering everything,' Peg said judiciously as she nibbled on her lip, 'I believe I'll have—oatmeal. What do we hear from Jim—er—Mr Marston?'

'He decide to get up today,' Bea said. 'So I show him the bathroom, and——'

The shout of anguish almost shook the house. 'And you forgot to tell him we only have cold water,' Peg giggled. 'Oh, well, it ought to wake him up.'

'If it don't kill him first,' Bea added. 'You know, you gotta watch out for that man, love. He ain't no village boy, you know. Somethin' about him worries me. Eyes, maybe. He always looks as if he can see inside you, huh?'

And that's exactly right, Peg told herself. That's just what makes me feel so uneasy about that man. He *can* see inside my head! All my foolish, mixed-up dreams. I'm convinced he knows them all! 'But he's a good-looking man,' she teased, as she snatched up a slice of the freshly buttered toast and started to nibble on it.

Bea grinned at her, the gold tooth in the very centre of her mouth gleaming for all it was worth. 'Yeah, you got that right, child,' the housekeeper said. 'You and him—you'd have beautiful children!'

'Bea!'

'Well, ain't no use trying to bury you head in the sand,' Bea muttered as she turned back to the hot stove. 'That's what life is all about, girl. Man and woman and children!'

'I suppose it is.' Peg sighed as she sat down in the chair and put both elbows on the table. 'Mighty hard to arrange when there aren't any young men within ten miles of the place.'

'Don't stop nobody from dreamin',' Bea reminded her. 'Here. Eat you oatmeal.' Peg looked down at the steaming dish as her hand automatically added two spoonfuls of sugar and a drop or two from the milk pitcher. Goat's milk, of course. Cows were doing well at the other end of the island, in the relatively more gentle Mesopotamia Valley, and on Young Island, the tourist island just off Kingstown, but up here in the real mountains cattle could not live—and goats could.

So she dreamed, as she spooned up the food. Peggy Mitchell, Queen of the World, sitting on her lounger with a dozen very masculine servants running at her beck and call. Or Mrs Peggy Something—surrounded by half a dozen little children, all with brown hair and lovable...hazel eyes? It was hard to hide the blush, and the attempt almost made her choke on the oatmeal. So, while she coughed and choked and bent over trying to catch her breath, that was when Jim Marston *had* to come in, of course!

'Good morning, all.'

Peg glanced up and then ducked her head. Freshly shaved and showered, dressed in shirt and shorts and bare feet, he took her breath away. And made her realise how ratty her hair looked, tied back with a shoestring. Not a trace of make-up, and dressed in her oldest blouse and slacks, and— 'Oh, God,' she groaned.

'Something I said?' He was behind her chair before she knew it, one hand resting on her shoulder. She could feel the heat of him burning right through her blouse.

'Mus' not have made the oatmeal too smooth,' Bea offered, the sarcasm about three layers thick as she spoke.

Peg reached blindly for her coffee-mug, and managed to get a little of the hot liquid down her throat. Jim pulled up a chair opposite her, but the little round kitchen table was so small that his feet became entangled with her own. Another blush, and a quick movement backwards, as he grinned at her. Damn man, she thought!

'What you want for breakfas', man?' Bea waddled over to the table, put both hands on her hips, and defied him to do his worst. He did.

'Eggs, ham, toast, coffee, orange juice,' he ordered, as if he were sitting in his favourite restaurant.

'OK. Takes a minute,' Bea answered, and made off towards the stove.

'But——' Peggy started to protest.

'He a big man,' her housekeeper told her, waving a wooden spatula for emphasis. 'Can't live on no oatmeals for breakfast!'

'Oatmeal? You have oatmeal?'

'Got three sixty-pound sacks,' Bea confided. 'Gettin' old, too. Mr Mitchell, he buys like that. Imported oatmeal. Imported flour for bread. If we don' eat it up pretty quick it all spoils! Fool man!'

'Your father, I take it?' He looked over at Peggy, the grin gone.

She nodded. 'Bea and my father, they never did see eye to eye.'

'Never did see why my lady marries that—drunk.' Bea was back with a dish piled high with scrambled eggs. 'Never had no gumption. Her father put up with him for a year, and then throwed him out of the house, he did. And my lady, too. Don't come back unless you comes without that miserable excuse for a man, he yells. And he don' write, don' answer telephone—nothin'. His only chick, she was, an' he cuts her out of his life. Hard old man, but honest! Never even got to see his granddaughter. Maybe he don' even know he gots one. Bitter old man. Don' got no orange juice this mornin'. That be papaya juice. You'll like it.'

'Bea!'

'What? He likes the juice, no?'

'I don't mean the juice,' Peg said, with a voice cold enough to freeze the Panama Canal. 'You talk too much, old woman!'

'Only thing I got left to do,' Bea responded. 'Posted the banns three times, I did. Married them all. Buried them all. Now I ain't got nothin' left by my little baby here.' She slouched out of the room, her slippers making slapping noises as counterpoint to her grumbling.

'I'm sorry about that,' Peg said after a moment's pause.

'No need to be.'

'She helped raise my mother, and she raised me, and—there isn't much I can do to make her stop.'

'No need to explain.' He toasted her in his coffee-mug. 'I wish I had a half-dozen people like her around me. Loyalty is hard to come by. And I love oatmeal, by the way.'

Almost like a robot, so strict had been her training, Peg was up out of her chair and at the stove before she even thought what she was doing. When it struck her hands stopped in mid-air and she looked back over her shoulder. 'You mean that?'

'Of course.'

She could not help but grin as she reached for the cold water, and transformed the dried cereal into a hot meal. As she stirred the mix over the flame, she thought. He was a big handsome man. Not too old at all, although not too young, either. I wonder what he does in New York? Without a guard on her tongue the words tumbled out.

'Me?' He tasted the oatmeal and accepted the syrup she passed him.

'Honey,' she said. 'The last of our own honey. Coffee-flavoured. You'll like that, too.'

'I have a business in New York,' he explained. 'Exporting and importing. That sort of thing. This *is* tasty honey. You haven't any more?'

'No, not a bottle. My father—well, Mr Marston, my father wasn't cut out to be a farmer. A couple of years ago he cut down all our coffee trees. We still have the bees, but there's nothing better than honey made from coffee flowers. You were saying?'

'Was I?'

'About the exports and imports. I suppose you own a lot of warehouses and ships and things like that?'

'Not a bit.' He grinned at her over his spoon. A sort of shark's grin, were she to know it. Here it comes, he told himself. Oh, and what do you do with your millions, Mr Marston? 'No, nothing,' he continued. 'My organisation serves as a middleman. We find people with something to sell, and look around for someone who wants to buy that particular something, and we arrange for them to get together. For which, of course, they pay us a nominal fee.' At this point, he told himself, she says something about, Oh, you must have an interesting life, and I'll bet you make a great deal of money!

Instead of which she thumped both elbows down on the table and sighed. 'Lord, I wish I had known you two years ago,' she murmured. 'I would have loved to have been able to hire you. At a nominal fee, of course.'

He couldn't hold back. Curiosity, not black magic, was what had led him into a thousand dark corners, out of which he had come clutching more millions. Curiosity, a tremendous memory, and enough available cash to back up his every endeavour. 'Want to tell me about it?' he asked.

'It's a long story,' she said. 'Let me top up your coffee.' He pushed the mug in her direction as she filled it and settled back. 'My father was always the sort of man who would go to extremes,' she said. 'He cut down the coffee trees—oh, I don't dispute that. Coffee was selling so low nobody could make a profit. But instead he put in arrowroot!'

Jim's memory search went into high gear, and found nothing labelled arrowroot. Peg watched him, cradling her mug between her hands. She could almost see the gears turning behind his hazel eyes, but he was coming up all lemons, evidently.

'Arrowroot,' she prompted. 'It produces the most digestible starch in the world. Manufacturers used it worldwide for baby foods and health diets and things like that.'

Jim shrugged his shoulders. 'All I can remember is that the market dropped dead,' he said. 'What happened?'

'What always happens when the price goes up too high,' she told him. 'Some smart *jaboo* went into his laboratory and invented a chemical substitute at half the price!'

'Ah! And that was the year your father decided to go into arrowroot?'

'The very time,' Peg said. 'You couldn't give the stuff away two years ago. Everyone in St Vincent switched out of arrowroot into peanuts, things like that. Not my pop. Bound to come back, he insisted. So we planted another crop of arrowroot last year. We had so many tons of arrowroot in storage that it wasn't even funny. So this year, when planting time came around again——'

'Don't tell me,' he said soberly. 'More arrowroot?'

'Bumper crop,' Peg admitted wryly. 'Two hundred acres of it. If anyone finds a market for the stuff, we'll make a fortune!'

His mind was working overtime. Somewhere recently he had read or heard a conversation. All he needed to do was remember. And Vera Helst, sitting down there in Kingstown—or out looking for him, perhaps. Lord, what a sting *this* would make! But be cautious, man!

'You don't *look* like a bankrupt, Peggy.' It was the first time he had used her name in discussion. A little chill ran up her spine. Or maybe it was fire. She couldn't quite decide.

'No, not quite.' She laughed, a low contralto chuckle that filled the room. 'No, I argued so hard and long that my father compromised. He kept the two hundred acres and his arrowroot, and I formed a co-operative and put the other eighty-eight acres into things that would either sell to the tourist hotels, or could be eaten for ourselves. Carrots, string beans, lima beans, bok-choy—the Chinese cabbage—and onions. This year our breadfruit trees started to yield, and our aubergine came in. No, we're not bankrupt. We're not getting rich, either. We're hanging in there, just ahead of the mortgage payments. Oh, and I should mention that our Co-operative runs two fishing boats, and the sea is full of fish. And that, sir, is the end of my lecture. Next year, no arrowroot will be planted. I don't want to overwhelm you with the size of our disaster.'

'Only you wish that brother Andrew would hurry home?' Her head snapped up as she stared at him. Mind-reading? Dear heaven, how does he know?

'Maybe you'd like to come out and walk the farm with me,' she proposed, to get him off *that* subject.

Bea came bustling back in at just that moment. She's been standing outside the door listening all this time,

Peggy told herself, and then laughed at her own fears. Poor Bea. My watchdog, no less.

'You remember what I tole you,' the housekeeper told him as he got up and stretched. 'Missy, you better find him a big hat. He gotta big head, that man.' Peg, who knew when she was being told to go, grinned at both of them and went out hat-hunting.

'I remember,' he assured Bea as he shook his head gently. 'Hands in my pockets. Do I have to whistle at the same time?'

'And there it all is.' Peggy waved her arm in a vague half-circle around the horizon. There was hardly a flat piece of land to be seen, but everywhere the tall string bushes with their oblate green leafs and tiny white flowers filled the landscape. In the distance a couple of men from the village were pulling up the bulbous roots, sampling the crop. Satan, drafted to carry the lunch basket, nibbled on the occasional weed.

'Well!' he commented, as he pushed his borrowed hat back and scratched his head. 'It's not what I thought. I've always imagined miles and miles of flat fields, "amber waves of grain", that sort of thing. You've got the stuff growing over hill and dale—even out from the sides of the cliffs!'

'All the easier to harvest,' she laughed. 'This is the West Indian arrowroot. *Maranta arundinacea*, you know.'

'No, I don't know,' he chuckled. 'But you sound as if you do?'

'Well, of course,' she returned. 'Did you think I was a know-nothing? My father was a fine botanist. And my brother is studying the science of agriculture, not just the practice. I suppose I might go Stateside to study after Andrew takes over, but—I don't know that my heart is really in farming. Maybe I'll go into nursing full time. I've always meant to study further, but what with one thing and another, I——'

'Your mother, I suppose, was a great handicap?' She didn't seem embarrassed by the question, but nodded her head.

'Yes, Mother was a handicap to my career, in one sense, but then again, I don't know. I nursed her for four years, you know. I think it taught me a lot. I used to be a weepy wimp. But that isn't all. My brother is a brilliant scholar, while I'm just—not cut from the same cloth. Somebody had to stay at home, and I was the only girl—and there you have it.' She gave a dry, hesitant chuckle, and turned away from him.

For a moment he made no answer. They were sitting on the donkey's ornate blanket, while Satan nibbled and wandered in a circle around them.

Peggy, not at all disturbed by the conversation, was staring out over the Caribbean when the warm strong arm came around her. It didn't exactly startle her; she was a great one for daydreams, and was pursuing one in which Jim Marston was prominently involved when he made his move. Gently the arm pulled her back until she was resting against his chest.

A nice feeling, she told herself, as the softness of her seemed to melt into the iron muscles of his chest. His fingers flicked at the shoestring tie at the nape of her neck and her hair blew loosely out into the onshore breeze. She turned her head and looked up at him over her shoulder. He was looking out to sea, brooding, and it was hard to tell what he was thinking about.

'I don't see that,' he said in his deep, soft voice. 'No way you would have been a wimp, Peggy. Look around you. Busy people working, earning their keep because of your inspiration.'

She turned her head to rest against his chest, and chuckled.

'I said something funny?'

'Not really. I *do* apologise. Only it's high noon, Jim. If you look around you won't find a soul working at anything.'

'Well, I'll be—I didn't even hear the quitting whistle.'

'Folk around here don't need a whistle, massa,' she teased. 'Nobody works in the noonday sun. That line of yours will be great a couple of hours from now. Our people work like the devil when it's time; and they play like the devil when it's time.'

'And right now it's time for what?'

'Napping,' she told him. 'Care to join me?'

'That's the best offer I've had yet.' He gradually shifted her weight off his shoulder and stretched out beside her.

'Sleeping, that's all I'm offering,' she said hesitantly.

'What else is there?' he chuckled. 'Come on, now.'

She examined him with a jaundiced eye. A great deal of man, stretched out on her dusty blanket, capable of— what? Her medical training had left her few mysteries in the way of men and their needs, but it was all theoretical. And there was nothing theoretical about this man. Close enough to touch. And not being able to help herself, she did. Her long, thin index finger reached out and tapped his aristocratic nose, and then ran down across his mouth and jumped off his chin.

'That's not exactly fair,' he rumbled. She laughed at him, and settled back on her elbow in the triangle between his arm and chest.

'Anything's fair,' she teased him. 'This is an equal opportunity world we live in.'

'Pardon me. I didn't know the rules.' He tugged at her elbow. The bend collapsed and she dropped on to his chest. His own finger came up to touch her own nose, trailed down across her mouth, off her chin, and landed on the peak of her instantly roused breast. She stopped breathing. There was such a rapid response that panic overwhelmed her. Panic and some sort of wild feeling she had never ever experienced.

His hand moved in a gentle circle, creating more havoc. Her blouse was light cotton, and she never wore a bra. It felt as if the fingers were on her flesh. And still she could neither breathe nor move. For a moment he toyed with her, his fingers probing between the buttons of her blouse, across the inflamed flesh. And then he seemed to notice.

'Dear God, woman, breathe!' he roared at her. His hands moved to her shoulders and shook. 'Breathe, damn you!' He jumped to his feet and dragged her with him. The air gusted into her lungs with a long sigh. She began to tremble all over. He cradled her in his arms. 'It's all right,' he murmured in her ear over and over. 'It's all right.' And just as suddenly as it had begun, it ended, and it *was* all right.

His voice dropped from hurricane force to a gentle whisper while he pulled her up against his chest and folded her into himself. Her head tucked in very nicely under his chin. She laid her cheek against him, and the thundering of his heart against her ear conquered all her fears. One of his hands was stroking her hair again, the other remained at the small of her back.

'Peggy. Miss Mitchell. I'm very sorry that I'm such a stupid man. Could you forgive me?'

She leaned back a little way, far enough back to see his face clearly. Concern was written deep in the furrows of his forehead. For some vague reason she felt as if she had known him all her life. There was no doubt of forgiveness in her mind, but she just could not muster the words. Instead she squirmed her hands and arms out from his bear-grip, and stretched up on tiptoes to clasp them around his neck.

'Funny little creature,' he murmured. 'Did you know that you're smiling and crying at the same time?' He bent his head and kissed her eyelids. 'There, that's better. Shall we start all over again?'

She blinked the tears and broadened her smile, still unable to produce words. His lips came down again— on hers. A gentle, warm, moist kiss, it lingered but for a moment, and then he drew back and gently pushed her a foot or two distant from himself, leaving his hands on her shoulders.

'Now then, Miss Mitchell,' he said briskly, 'tell me something more about this arrowroot business.'

He might have escaped any retribution, but Peggy, smiling, was knuckling her eyes at just the moment that Satan came wandering over to check up on the noise. The donkey's sharp eyes missed nothing. He went into a loping start, and raced the last few feet like an avenging angel. His lowered head, an imitation of all the goats among whom he lived, rapped Jim Marston right in the middle of his back.

Jim buckled forward, grabbing at Peg as he went. Wrapped in each other's arms, the pair of them went off the side of the hill, rolling like a ball down the gentle slope that led to the next ledge, about fifteen or twenty feet away from the top of the plateau.

The grass was thick. Neither was damaged a bit, except perhaps in his pride, Peg thought as she struggled to unwrap herself from the carnage. An ordinary man would roar at her now, blame everything on her. This one chuckled, stopped, and then broke out in an uproarious belly laugh that shook the pair of them. And shook Satan, too. The donkey had been standing above them peering down. Now he skittered his way back and forth down the hill and joined them.

'Why, you——' Jim started. The donkey brayed, a massively sharp tone that assaulted ears as much as five hundred yards away. Two of the foraging goats were drawn to the crest of the hill to add curiosity to their daily diet. Out of the corner of his eye Marston noted that Peggy was bent double, beside a couple of projecting rocks. 'Look what you've damn well done!' he yelled at the donkey. Another bray split the air. Holding his hands over his ears, Jim Marston abandoned the unequal cursing contest and went over to comfort the girl.

Peggy was indeed doubled up. When he came over and pulled her to her feet she buried her face in his shirt, and it was only then that he realised that she was laughing excessively at them both!

'But it wasn't very polite of you to laugh.' They had both climbed back up the hill, and were sitting at the edge of the cliff on Sunset Point, looking out to the west. The sandwiches Bea had provided had long since disappeared down a number of throats, including Satan's. Marston sounded as if his dignity had been affronted, but somehow Peggy knew he was teasing.

'Nobody ever died from laughter,' she answered haughtily. She had taken off her hat, and the cool ocean breeze scattered her curls, but did not erase them. They floated around her head like a halo. He seems to like that, she told herself, but that isn't the reason I did it. There's no reason why I should cater to his tastes, is there? Of course there isn't! Still, it never hurts to make friendly gestures, especially if they don't cost anything!

'Well, I almost did,' he mourned. 'I don't believe you have any idea how sharp the noise from your donkey is, close up.'

'I wouldn't know,' she told him, with a teasing smile on her face. 'He hasn't assaulted me in many a month. I love him, you see.'

'Yes, I can see that,' he returned, suddenly solemn. 'I suppose it's only proper that a donkey should try to defend its master. But then, I don't know a great deal about donkeys.'

'Or arrowroot,' she added, smiling.

'Or farms in the tropics,' he continued. Or women, the voice inside his head told him. You might have known a great deal about those females in New York, but out here in the sunlight, friend, playing roll-down-the-hill with this little lady, all of a sudden you've forgotten how much two and two make!

'I suppose——' she started to say, and then came to a stop. He looked down at her speculatively, and then changed the subject.

'This arrowroot,' he mused. 'It's a perennial flowering bush, and you have to pull it up when it goes dormant, shave the bulb, grind the shavings, and the powder is what's for sale?'

'Generally speaking,' she agreed. 'You've learned a lot today, haven't you? It isn't all that easy but that's the general idea.'

'And all this requires a considerable amount of labour, I suppose?'

'Very much so,' she agreed. 'Nobody has ever developed a machine system of harvesting. But the people are available, you know. The unemployment rate on this island is very high.'

'How would it be,' he wondered on, 'if I were to find some kind soul who would just like to purchase some of the most digestible form of starch in the world?'

'You have to be kidding,' she told him. 'Don't you think we've tried, these last few years? Not only me and my dad, but the whole darn government?'

'The British government?'

'No,' she murmured. 'That shows how much *you* know. St Vincent has been an independent country for years now! And you made a smart remark because I couldn't tell how far Chicago is from New York!'

'Ah, but then neither your government nor you know as much about world markets as I do,' he told her. 'I don't do it all by myself inside my narrow little head, you know. I maintain a research organisation in New York that knows more secrets per square yard than anybody you ever met!'

'I don't understand. Are you serious? You're really serious! You're just going to wander off and find some people who suddenly have a mad urge to buy my arrowroot. Just like that?'

'Well, perhaps not just like that,' he returned. 'It will take a little thought, a little concentrated research, a little role-playing.'

'Whoa!' she shouted at him. 'Stop right there. Role-playing?'

'Nothing to it,' he said, chuckling. 'I'm sure there are plenty of places—maybe right here on this island—with arrowroot to sell. So if I run down this somebody who wants to buy, you have to act as if your arrowroot is the best in the world. In a word, you have to have confidence in your product, and you have to show that confidence. Nothing wrong with that, is there?'

'I—no, I suppose not. It won't be much of an act. Because of the volcanic soil out here, our arrowroot *is* the best in the world. But you're suggesting some sort of—performance?'

'Yes and no. Nothing you couldn't handle, Peggy. You know I told you that I don't buy and sell for myself. I just put people who want to buy in contact with people who want to sell. That means *you* have to be prepared to defend the quality and the availability of your goods. They may want, for example, more than this one crop you have in the ground.'

'Oh, but I've got twice as much stored in the barns. All prime roots. But I haven't a grinding mill, and this year's crop would have to be harvested. I couldn't afford that separately, you know.'

'All to the good,' he assured her. 'You take the time to figure all that out. What grinding costs, what harvesting costs. Or, as an alternative, you can sell the roots as is. That's always a good ploy.'

'And—I wouldn't have any idea what to ask. If there's no market, how could I set a price?'

'These people aren't going to tell you *why* they want the stuff, Peg. The regular market has gone bust, so when I track somebody down it will be a group that will have a different prospect in mind, and they surely won't want to tell *you*. No, all you have to do is figure your costs for three years' worth of crops, and then double that figure——'

'A hundred-per-cent profit?' she gasped.

'Yes,' he said solemnly, but she could see the twinkle in his eye. 'I'm sure you could get more, but it doesn't pay to press your luck!'

But his thinking had gone far beyond Peggy's narrow education. She stood entranced, and said, 'Oh, my,' over and over again until he touched her shoulder again, and brought her back to earth.

'That's a curious reaction,' he commented as she caught her breath.

'What is?'

'Every time I touch you, you jump. Do you do that for all your men friends?'

'No, I don't,' she snapped, and then blushed at how much she had revealed. 'I mean—I'm not accustomed—I mean, you startled me when you did that, that's all!'

'Ah, a perfectly normal reaction. I suppose if I didn't surprise you you wouldn't jump?'

'Of course I wouldn't,' she told him indignantly, and then gasped, 'What are you doing?'

'Why, nothing at all,' he said mildly. 'I'm just giving advance notice so you won't be surprised. I'm going to kiss you.'

'Well, you certainly are not going——'

But by the time she got to the 'going' he was already going. His arms came around her, gently but firmly, and she didn't feel like struggling, anyway. His lips sealed her off from the world, warm, moist, comfortable. No, strike that out, her mind told her. Not comfortable—exciting! I have to ask him about that. But she was still, alas, running a mile behind him, and by the time she was ready to ask it was all over.

'See,' she managed to gasp. 'I didn't jump, did I?'

'No, indeed not,' he assured her. But *you* did, man, his conscience challenged him. He ignored it, and, as a man of considerable experience, he managed not to show it.

'This root you have in the ground, is it ready for harvest?' he asked.

'Almost overdue,' she sighed. 'You have some idea?'

'Lots of ideas,' he laughed. 'Life hasn't been this much fun in a long time. Look, do you think the farm—er—plantation could spare you for a couple of days?'

'I'm sure it could,' she allowed. 'I'm not the most important person in the world, not right this moment.'

'Then we'll go down to Kingstown, you and I.' He nodded his head and grinned, as if the last piece of his scheme had just fallen into place. 'I remember seeing someone down there that—just might—be interested. We would have to spend a couple of days. I'll make reservations at some hotel, I'll send some cables, and we can look round. Maybe you could give me the guided tour of the island. How about that?'

'I don't mind,' she said slowly. 'In fact, I'd love to do just that. Only there's Bea——'

'Of course. Mama Bear.'

'Well, she's been more than a mother to me. Don't you make fun of Bea.'

'But this is purely business. And if we're successful we'll set your plantation back on its feet—at least for a time. Nothing wrong with *that* for a goal, is there?'

'Not if you promise to keep your hands in your pockets,' she said, laughing. 'Yes, I'll go with you. But now it's late. Let's get Satan and get back to the house. I can't wait to tell Bea. And Henry! The village will be——'

'Hey,' he cautioned. 'Not everybody in the wide world. This thing is a secret until we get a signature on the sales contract. Why won't this damn donkey come when I say come?'

'Because he's a free spirit and you're trying too hard,' Peg chuckled. 'You must ask him politely. *De bonne grâce.*' Jim reluctantly released the halter and stepped back. Peggy assumed his former position directly in front of the animal, which was now sitting on its backside and glaring. She spoke softly, extending her hand. The little beast considered for a moment, then struggled awkwardly to his feet and stood both docile and ready.

'So,' Jim Marston chuckled. 'You can lead a donkey to water——

'Not exactly,' Peggy confessed. 'I reminded him that the truck was going to the glue factory next week. Help me put that blanket on him, will you? He can carry the empties back down.'

The trip back to the house went more quickly than the outward voyage. The two of them seemed more content, as if some working agreement had been achieved out there on the face of the mountain, which made a couple out of two strangers. Bea met them at the screen door.

'Ah, you have come back safely,' the old lady commented, staring directly at Jim Marston as if to demonstrate how much she had doubted such an ending to the day.

'Did you think we wouldn't?' Peggy giggled. 'We had a fine day, and Mr Marston—er—Jim is working out something that might help us sell the arrowroot crop. Isn't that clever?'

'They say in island school, beware Greeks bearing gifts,' Bea retorted. 'He look Greek. Or Eye-talian. You took you hat off again out in the sun, missy. How many times I tell you the sun makes freckles! Hurry up, now. Dinner is almost ready. Something special.'

The three of them gathered an hour later at table, where the something special turned out to be a fresh roasted pork shoulder. 'That old sow don't breed no more,' Bea explained. 'So when Henry come back from the city he brings us a shoulder. It's the way of the world. Nice pork, though.'

'But dangerous,' Peggy cautioned. Jim looked up at her with a questioning look. 'No refrigeration,' she explained. 'Pork picks up trichinosis. It must be thoroughly cooked to avoid the danger.'

'My favourite food,' he moaned. 'You people lead me to believe living in the tropics is dangerous to your health!'

'Only if you don't obey the rules,' Peg teased. 'Eat moderately, exercise moderately, and boil everything, especially the water. Now, we go to Kingstown tomorrow?'

'As early as possible,' he agreed. But his smile faded quickly when he saw Bea's face.

'What's this!' the old woman demanded suspiciously.

'A business trip,' Peg interjected quickly. 'A couple of days, to see if we can line up buyers for the crop.'

'Better I come with you,' Bea said doggedly. 'We leave Ada in charge of the plantation.'

'No, that's not necessary,' Peggy insisted firmly. 'You know you hate to travel on that rickety bus, and you know that I'm all grown-up now, Bea!'

'Yes. That's the trouble,' the old lady insisted. 'You all grown up, missy.'

'Now that's enough,' Peggy snapped. 'It's a business trip, pure and simple, and Mr Marston and I are going!'

Bea grumbled for the rest of the evening, and they were all abed earlier than one would have expected, Bea to mumble, Jim Marston to scheme, and Peggy to dream.

Wild dreams. The sort of dreams that had no beginning and no end, but all seemed to indicate to her subconscious mind that the next day's trip might be neither pure nor simple, but would certainly be fun!

# CHAPTER THREE

LAST to sleep, first to awaken, Peggy slid out of her bed just as the cockerel outside sounded the first clarion call of dawn. There was light outside her window, but no sun. Wearily, she stretched and did a couple of limbering-up exercises before she wandered over to her dressing-table and peered into the mirror.

'Ugh!' she muttered, as she sank on to the stool and brushed aside the veil of silken red curls that floated in all directions around her head. Red hair, green eyes, skin and bone!

And the line of freckles was back, across her shoulders, the result of spending a day out in the sun without protective skin balm. In the sea of black faces that made up the population of St Vincent, the few white faces were forever in need of protection.

Restless, she took a quick peek into the hall to be sure that no adult males were about, then dodged down to the bathroom. The shower water was as cold as usual. The stream that brought it to the house started high up on the side of Mt Soufrière, in the clear, cool crater lake. She was half-dressed, drying and brushing her hair, when she heard the heavy thud of male boots parading down the hall. Well, they *had* to be male boots, didn't they? Only she and Jim Marston shared this wing of the house. Bea lived in a two-room suite on the other side of the kitchen.

As soon as the sound had passed her by she snatched up her nightgown, wrapped herself in a bath towel, and went back to her own bedroom. Her bag was packed—

49

done the night before, when she couldn't sleep and
packing seemed to be the only sensible thing to do. And
her travelling clothes were laid out. A simple cotton dress
in sunshine yellow, with a scooped neckline and a flaring
waist. Shoes to match, and nothing else. It didn't pay
to dress up in the tropics. And then down to the kitchen.

Jim was already sitting at the table; Bea was busy at
the stove. 'Pancakes,' the elderly housekeeper announced proudly. 'He like pancakes.'

'Don't I even get to choose?' she asked. Bea sniffed
at her. It was plain to see that when the male selected,
he chose for all! So unfair, Peggy told herself without
really meaning it. In fact, she had to stifle a giggle, and
almost choked doing it. Just supposing he was to hang
around here forever, she reflected. I'd have to make a
*lot* of adjustments in my life-style, wouldn't I? But *she*
liked pancakes too, so it wasn't a terrible doom!

'Nice outfit,' he commented, his mouth still working
on the pancake stack. She twirled around to show him
the whole effect. Just two words, and he had made the
sun shine. At least within the kitchen, he did.

'Do you really think so?'

'Really do. Didn't know they had such stylish stuff
way down here. Of course, it's what you put into a dress
that makes it special. That's special.' And he went back
to his pancakes.

The two women stared at each other over his head.
Bea wore a contemplative look, as if something he said
had touched a chord within her. He had touched a chord
in Peggy's mind, too—sheer astonishment.

'Don' see nothin' like that around here,' Bea said.
'Except for missy, of course. She made that dress up
from scratch. Cut and sewed and ironed and all. A fine
girl, my missy. Can do anything a woman ought to do!'
The housekeeper went to the stove and came back to set

a platter of steaming cakes on the table. 'Missy can do anything.'

'Yes, I can see that,' he returned, and the thought flashed through Peggy's mind that he sounded just the slightest bit sarcastic. But then, the twinkle was in his hazel eyes, it was altogether a lovely day, and he was— well, you didn't call a man lovely, did you? To cover her confusion she looked at the old-fashioned man's wrist- watch she wore.

'If we don't get a wiggle on, we'll miss the bus,' she announced.

'So why worry? We'll catch the next one. And bring enough for a day or two.' He looked at her startled expression and wondered what he had said this time to disturb her!

'You miss this bus,' Bea explained, 'an' the next one come on Friday. Bring enough what?'

'Clothing. We'll probably want to stay overnight, maybe longer. It'll take a while for us to find our—to do all the errands we need to get done.'

'And, Peggy——' She stopped at the door to hear his last instruction.

'Find something sexy for the evenings!'

She arched her eyebrows at him as she left the kitchen. Behind her she could hear part of what Bea was saying: 'Hands in you pockets and whistle, man! Stay over- night, indeedy! All that making up with me, that ain't gonna help you!'

Peggy followed Jim down the trail, laughing to herself. It had been only three days ago that she had guided him in the other direction, a perfect stranger, with glassy eyes and an arrogant little frown. And now he bounded from rock to rock like a native goat—or maybe a satyr, she told herself as she hurried to keep up. In his khaki shorts and bush jacket he was a fine figure of a man, that one. Bea's long lecture came to her mind, ending with 'An' take care, missy. That man, he's trouble with a capital T, b'lieve me!'

'I believe, I believe,' she muttered as she trotted along behind him, and caught up as he reached the track that was the road.

'What?' She stumbled, and he saved her from a fall with easy strength, and a hearty laugh.

'Nothing,' she panted. 'I just believe—that you must be years younger than me.' Thankfully she leaned against him until she had caught her breath. There was a comfortable moment, and then his arm came over her shoulder, reminding. She whirled away with a laugh, stumbled again, and sat down hard on a solid piece of lava-rock by the roadside.

'Ha,' he joked. 'Softy. Me Tarzan, you Peg!' He drummed on his chest with both hands, and then feigned a sudden pain and a cough.

'Come on now,' she teased. 'I saw that movie when we lived in Puerto Rico, and that was years ago. Thank you for carrying my bag.'

'Think nothing of it.' He looked north and south, along the track of the road which, at this point, was merely a pair of ruts. 'The bus comes from up there? What the devil exists north of here?'

'Just a trail,' she answered, bending over to dig a pebble out of her shoe. 'A few villages, and a few farms like ours. But it doesn't go all the way around the cliffs. There's a break, and then there's Fancy.'

'Fancy?' He gave her a look that said, 'Stop-pulling-my-leg.'

'It's a town,' she insisted. 'And it's connected all the way around the other side of the island by the Windward Highway. Only you——'

'I know,' he chuckled. 'Only you can't get there from here because of the cliffs and—good lord, is that the bus?'

Peggy got up gracefully, watching his face, and enjoying the play of emotions that ran across it. It *was* the bus. How could anyone miss it? An old Ford truck, so old that it could be classified as ancient, painted orange and red. Behind the unroofed cab a staked body was filled with four long wooden benches, running the length of the vehicle, with barely enough room for passengers to squeeze by. Equipped by law to hold twenty, it had thirty-two occupants already, and squeeze-room for more.

The machine clattered to a halt and a young man helped them up the rickety ladder. Jim looked round at the sea of black and brown faces, mostly women, all looking him over. 'I don't think there's a seat to be had,' he muttered to her.

'Nonsense,' Peggy insisted. And, sure enough, everyone on the already crowded truck seemed to squeeze an inch or two in different directions, and there, amid grins, was seating space for two. They had to move quickly; the truck was already in gear when the seats appeared, and jerked forward strongly enough to throw them both into the arms of their neighbours.

'Eh, missy.' The very robust woman with Peggy in her arms helped her to squeeze in, and then the good-natured barrage began. 'Missy, that one fine man you caught, eh? Where you get him?'

'He fell off the road,' Peg laughed, dropping into the native patois. 'And I *cotched* him. Nice? Look at those muscles.' She held up his right arm so all the travellers could see. There were oohs of appreciation.

'Hey, wait a darn minute,' he muttered.

'Don't fight it,' she murmured in his ear. 'It's the way. You wouldn't want them to think you were a Kingstown snob, would you?'

'Pretty scrawny,' the old woman across from them noted. 'Maybe you better throw him back.'

'Or maybe I take him off your hands,' the first woman chimed in. When she laughed there was so much of her that she seemed to jiggle in several directions at once.

'And now what do you say?' he chuckled softly.

'Don't get in over your head,' Peggy muttered, and then to the crowd, 'I need to think. He's nice to look, but does that fill the pot?'

'Ah, no job?' the old woman asked sadly. 'But—you know, missy, until you get hungry, man like that could be lots of fun. Me, I know. Besides, he don't know nothin' to work, he can always push and shove. Keep him for week or two!'

'What the devil does that mean?' he asked cautiously.

'Nothing bad,' she grinned. 'Push and shove. Hoe and shovel. You could do that, couldn't you?'

'Girl like you, got your own farm and all, you can afford to keep him on just for the night work,' their neighbour suggested.

'And now tell me why you're blushing,' he murmured as she turned to him and buried her crimson cheeks in his jacket.

'Shut up,' she whispered. 'Just shut up!' A great cackle of laughter filled the truck, and the conversation turned to the next pair to board.

Somehow, in the general shifting and movement, his arm came around her shoulder. 'Even Bea couldn't expect me to keep my hands in my pockets in this crowd,' he murmured.

'I suppose not,' she relented, 'but you remember we all expect you to be very circumspect if we're going to be business partners!' And with her priorities all straight, she snuggled against him—for the comfort and support, since the benches had no backs, of course.

'Business partners?' he wondered, and then gave her a little squeeze. 'Oh, arrowroot. Yeah. Of course.'

The truck lurched southwards, found the end of the paved road, bounced up on it, and rushed at madcap speed over the river bridge and by Châteaubelair, while the passengers gossiped, sang, snapped, breast-fed babies, exchanged recipes, and good-naturedly injected themselves into their neighbours' problems and successes.

'And they all know you?' he murmured in her ear.

'Well, we've lived here for some time,' she explained, 'and they're a friendly people. They understand life, and they know that nobody is perfect. I can remember when I went crying to Auntie Bess—that lady over there—when my father came home drunk once too often. "Every man," she told me, "got a right to go to hell in his own way. Jus' see you don't go all the way with him!"'

'Some advice!' he snorted. 'That kind of friend you don't need.'

'Yes, I do,' she returned fiercely. 'While she was telling me that she was also helping to clear up the house after Papa practically knocked the place down. And her husband, that skinny little man beside her, he replanted the vegetable garden for us that Satan tore up that same night! They're good and loving people. Just because they like to speak their own minds doesn't turn me off!' She sniffed, and tried to draw away from him, but there wasn't enough room in the truck. Besides, she told herself, I really don't want to move!

'So tell me something about them,' he suggested. 'All I ever read about the island is what's on the navigation charts.'

'Well, there's not much to tell,' she sighed. 'There are perhaps eighty-five thousand people here. But the birth rate is so high, and the emigration rate fluctuates, and nobody really knows for sure. They're the descendants of African slaves, with a mixture of Scots and French and English. Most are farmers or fishermen. Somehow the tourist trade has never quite touched the island. Practically all the Carib Indians are long gone, although there are some few Black Caribs in the mountains. This island and a few of the small Grenadines used to be part of an Associated State—with Britain—but it acquired full independence within the Commonwealth in 1979. There's a parliamentary system with a Prime Minister, and the Governor-General represents the Queen. Kingstown is the capital. All right?' The last phrase barely tumbled out.

'Bound to be,' he murmured into her hair as he drew her closer and settled her head on his shoulder. The fresh air, the lulling motion of the bus, the lack of sleep the night before, had all conspired against her, and Peggy fell fast asleep, with a broad smile on her face. What he could not know was that her dreams were filled by him, and bright moonlight sparkled on peaceful waters as they talked and sang and played together and did—whatever it was that a young couple did on warm tropical nights.

While Peggy napped, the truck trundled up and down on the corrugated road, through the lush tropical vegetation that seemed ready to reclaim the road at a moment's notice. It stopped anywhere a prospective passenger waved, discharged people and freight—especially live chickens—and spread song and conversation throughout an ever-changing passenger list, until finally it wandered around the flank of Mt St Andrew, and Kingstown lay before it.

The capital of St Vincent and the Grenadines might, on a market day, contain thirty thousand residents. Along the waterfront a line of stark warehouses cut off the view. Among its twenty or more streets people lived and died, transacted all life's business, went in out of the rain, and lived for the day. From the wide mouth of the bay the city filled the little mountain cove, backed by Dorsetshire Hill, moving from warehouse district to civic centre to more modern housing. But the bus steamed to a stop in the central park, parked itself directly in front of St George's, the Anglican cathedral, and shuddered into silence.

'Peggy?' He shook her gently. The rest of the travellers had dismounted and gone almost like a wave of water when the tailgate was dropped. Now the pair of them sat alone in the centre of the truck, and the driver, chewing a tender stalk of sugar-cane, was standing up in his roofless cab, smiling at them.

'Peggy?' Another shake. She groaned an objection, and wrapped both her hands around his arm, then snuggled closer on his shoulder. 'Peggy Mitchell!'

'That's not really my name.' She had managed to open one eye, and smiled up at him, not sure of just where they were. When she saw the old baroque tower of the cathedral over his shoulder she gasped, snapped to attention, and moved an inch or two away. 'Did I——?'

'All the way,' he laughed as he rubbed his arm. 'I think I may have to have my arm amputated.'

'Oh, I *am* sorry!' She sidled back to him, and joined in the rubbing.

'Hey, that's enough!' He stood up, stretching.

She rose with him. It was not her *arm* that ached. Twenty road-miles on a hard wooden bench had a more fundamental effect on her, but a *lady* would hardly rub that section in public. She could almost hear Bea threatening her, just at the thought!

'So Peggy isn't your name?' By dint of much urging he had manhandled her to the back of the truck, and vaulted to the ground effortlessly before turning around to pluck her out. Both his hands at her waist managed almost to encircle it. It gave her a delicious little thrill, and she almost complained when, her feet solidly on the pavement, he left her to her own devices.

'No,' she assured him as she brushed down her dress. 'Margarita Eloise Melinda Elizabeth Julia. That's what my birth certificate says. My dad had a pile of spinster aunts, and nobody expected me to live longer than twenty-four hours, so——'

'Peggy,' he chuckled. 'I'll stick to the simplistic solution. Now——' He stopped for a moment to get his bearings straight. 'The Blue Caribbean Hotel?'

'This-a-way,' she laughed, tucking her hand in his arm and tugging him into movement.

'Hey, the luggage,' he protested. Their two bags were sitting on the pavement looking rather forlorn.

'Not to worry,' she offered. 'First of all, the hotel will be glad to send porters to pick them up. Secondly, nobody would dare to steal them when the entire police force is watching.' She gestured grandly down to the corner, where a pair of uniformed officers were carrying on a conversation. 'And, thirdly, if someone *did* steal them, how would he get off the island? There isn't another aeroplane until tomorrow, nor a boat until next Tuesday!'

'OK, I get the message.' They walked across the square, idling. Jim Marston had seen someone standing on the steps of the church. It was Steve Shariek, the rather obese enquiry agent he had spotted and dodged when he had first landed. He pulled Peggy closer. 'Remember what I said about acting?' he whispered. She looked up at him, frowning.

'Now's the time. Curtain going up.'

'Now? I——'

'A little more adoration in the eyes,' he prompted. 'That's it. Snuggle the head on my arm—there's a good girl. Now we can go on. Remember, you're mad about me!'

'Mad *at* you, more than likely,' she said crossly. 'Do I simper a little? What in the world's going on? Some creditor of yours chasing you?'

'Not exactly, but you're getting close,' he laughed. 'The little fat guy. Don't walk too fast. I don't think he's capable of much speed, and I wouldn't want him to lose us.'

'I wish I knew what you're talking about,' she protested. But not too strongly. It would not, she told herself, take a great deal of effort to be mad over this man. Which is all the more reason, Peggy Mitchell, that you need to watch your step! Forewarned, she offered him a sunny smile, and led him in the direction of St Mary's, the Catholic cathedral that stood adjacent to St George's. Only an old graveyard separated the two massive buildings.

'That's some church,' he offered, as they wandered down the connecting path.

'St George's?' she giggled. 'Old enough. 1820, or something like that. A Regency church. In fact, they have a chandelier inside that was a gift of George III. Glittering——'

'Gold?' he interrupted.

'Not likely,' she said. 'Brass.'

'Well, I'll be——!' He stopped, forcing her to do the same.

'It's not all that important,' she told him. 'In fact, nobody's positive that the King did donate the thing. Especially since he died in January of 1820, and had been mad as a hatter since 1811. It's just a local——'

'I wasn't concerned about the church,' he muttered. 'Smell the air.'

Puzzled, she took a deep breath. Woodsmoke was about the only pollutant in St Vincent, so she could enjoy the gentle fragrances with which flowerbeds and trees perfumed the air.

'Nice, isn't it?' she said tentatively. He looked down at her as if she had suddenly become a congenital idiot.

'Nice? Is that all you've got to say? Nice? Lady, there's a fortune in that air. Can't you smell those trees?'

'Almond trees.' Her voice wavered. It was the first time she had ever seen him in action. He had suddenly come alive, like a hunter spotting his prey. Even his ears seemed to have swung slightly forward. 'They've been there for years,' she sighed, not knowing what else to say. 'Now if you want to see something interesting, we'll go over to the Botanical Gardens. There are some bread-fruit trees that Captain Bligh brought back from his second trip to the South Seas. Not in the *Bounty*. Later, in the *Providence*. And the trees are still alive, and——'

'Stop babbling,' he commanded. 'I don't care if Mr Christian dedicated the first church here. Let me think!'

'But I——'

'Let me think, dammit!'

'If you're going to be *that* mean about it, I might as well go——'

'Hey, I'm sorry.' There was an ornate iron bench a few feet down the path. He ushered her to it and sat her down, standing in front of her like an elderly curate about to raise a little hell and damnation in front of a wayward parishioner. 'Now I am about to read to you from the book of St Vincent,' he said ponderously.

'Thank you very much,' she said angrily. 'There's no such book.'

'There is now, Peggy Mitchell,' he said quietly. 'What's the difference between a poor man and a rich man?'

'Money,' she snapped. 'Now could we——'

'Not quite right,' he said, dropping on to the bench beside her. It wasn't a very *big* bench, and he was a very big man, crowding her personal space. Dominating, she thought, but he's not going to dominate me! She shifted as far as the bench allowed, and glared up at him.

'There's money everywhere in the world,' he pronounced, as if these were really words from the Good Book. 'The difference between a rich man and a poor one is that the rich man can recognise profit no matter what its form. Now—almonds. They grow well in St Vincent?'

'Everything grows well here,' she said firmly, and a little defiantly. 'We have a few behind the house, back on our farm. Everybody has them. So what?'

'Sweet almonds?' he asked suspiciously.

'Is there some other kind?'

'Bitter almonds,' he said truculently. She laughed.

'I thought that was only in Agatha Christie novels. The detective knows she's poisoned because her breath smells of bitter almond!'

'Come off it,' he threatened. 'This is no detective story. The poison is prussic acid. And it smells like bitter almonds because that's where it comes from, from the bitter almond tree. When they dehydrate it they get cyanide. Now, any more wise remarks?'

'I don't think so,' she muttered angrily. 'Just because you know all about almonds—how do you know?'

'Because when I read something I retain it,' he snorted. 'So now let's widen your horizons.' And then, in a softer tone which confused her more than his anger, he added, as he tilted up her chin with one huge finger, 'Did you know that you're beautiful when you're angry?'

She glared up at him, not knowing whether to laugh or cry, whether to kiss or bite. Her hand came up halfway, as if to slap his face, but he took her wrist gently and kissed her open palm. 'Mustn't forget the audience,' he told her. 'And in case you doubt it, you are beautiful, missy, audience or no.'

'I don't know what to make of you,' she admitted candidly. 'I'm really not—I——!' He kissed her palm again, throwing her completely off balance.

She struggled for a moment to re-establish control. 'About the olives,' she rasped, her voice clogged with emotions.

'Almonds,' he chuckled. 'The way you make a lot of money, missy, is to find something a lot of people want, and sell it to them for more than it cost you.'

'I've heard that said.' She ducked her head to hide the confused look that spread across her face.

'Then you should know,' he rumbled, more softly than before, 'that a great deal of the world's money is held in Japan. And there's nothing the Japanese like better than sweet almonds. They eat the nuts, use the oils—everything. And they pay top dollars for good stuff. So high is their requirement that they are actually buying up almond farms in California.' He stopped to put one arm around her shoulders. 'Now, after we get rid of the surplus arrowroot crop, what could be better than setting two hundred acres in almond trees?'

'Why, I—why, I don't know,' she gasped. 'I never thought of that! It would take some time for the trees to bear, of course, but—you really *are* a genius, aren't you!'

Exuberantly, with happy tears still trickling down her cheeks, she threw herself at him, landing up twisted across his lap, her arms around his neck, her lips seeking his. For a second he acted surprised, then a big grin flashed across his face and he leaned over to complete the connection.

Several minutes later, when he carefully disposed of a considerably dishevelled Peggy Mitchell by setting her down gently on the bench, he looked round. 'Well, our snoop got himself an eyeful,' he laughed. 'And I gather he's gone off to report. That's what I call good acting!'

'Yes,' she stammered, completely flustered by her own actions, his reactions, and their mutual response to a soul-searing kiss. 'Yes. That was good—acting, I mean. I think we'd better go on to the hotel.'

'Lovely place, here,' he suggested. 'We could sit for a time. I don't think the Bishop would be insulted?'

'I—couldn't possibly,' she muttered, struggling to her feet. 'The hotel's only a little way down the street, and——' And if I sit here another minute I'm going to fall completely into a pile of very tiny pieces, and do something that Bea would completely disapprove of!

The receptionist was glad to see them. There were three or four people in the lobby of the hotel, all of them asleep. 'Of course we can put you up,' he said, in a de-lightful English accent that barely concealed the rolling patois. 'A room for you and your lady——'

A sharp-pointed shoe nudged Jim Marston's ankle. 'Two rooms,' he said apologetically. 'Adjoining, of course.'

'Of course,' the clerk chattered happily. 'Now, the rainy season rates are in effect, and you can——'

'What's the difference in seasonal rates?' Jim asked casually.

The clerk sighed. 'Nothing,' he returned. 'But tourists never ask. The rates are on the American plan, no meals included. We have our own dining-room, and——'

'Telephones?'

'I—er—can find you a room with a telephone,' the clerk insisted. 'We have a considerable number of vacancies.'

'How many rooms, exactly, are vacant?'

'Er—eighteen,' he sighed. 'Your luggage will be picked up immediately. There is plenty of water this month, and——'

'You were very rude to him,' Peggy lectured a few minutes later as the door closed behind the elderly bellman. 'The reception clerk. You embarrassed him. They only have eighteen rooms in the hotel, Mr Marston!'

'Look,' he sighed, 'I'm sorry. I'm sorry for every bad deed I've ever done. I'm sorry for all the world's ills. I'm sorry that you don't like me today. I'm sorry that you didn't like me yesterday. I'll call down to the desk and apologise. Or would you rather I threw open a window and yelled an apology to the whole world?' He took two threatening steps in her direction.

'I think I'll take the other room and have a bath,' Peggy squeaked, as she jumped across the threshold through the connecting door and ran for the bathroom. She heard him laugh even though the door was closed behind her. Closed and locked. For all her vaunted coolness, Peggy Mitchell wasn't sure whether that was a friendly Green Giant laugh, or the 'Fee fi fo fum' of that other giant. She turned the water on full spate, and let the noise of the plumbing drown his telephone conversations.

# CHAPTER FOUR

'Look, it's Friday afternoon,' Peggy told Jim Marston in her most exasperated tone. 'Didn't I do enough, hanging on your every word last night at the dinner table? Trying to look as if I believed everything you said?'

'Last night didn't count,' he insisted, hurrying her along with one hand under her elbow. 'Besides, that food was so——'

'Spicy,' she interjected quickly, before he thought of some word with worse connotations. 'Spicy. The people on this island like spicy food. You *did* enjoy the callalo soup? And the sweet-potato pudding? And you drank enough of those *gris-gris* swizzles to sink the *Titanic*. Those were almost one-hundred-per-cent rum, you know!'

'I enjoyed everything,' he grimaced. 'Only they couldn't keep my water glass refilled. My tongue was in such trouble I couldn't tell whether you were looking at me adoringly or not! Where the devil is the post office?'

'Across the street.' She waved at the building where mail, telephone, and cable terminals were all provided. 'Her Majesty's postal service, Grenadine style.'

Grumbling, he led her a merry chase against the flow of traffic, and to her surprise avoided the post office completely, going instead up the steps of Barclay's bank.

'You'll kill yourself,' she muttered as he almost forced her on to one of the marble benches. 'Traffic goes on the left around here. You keep looking in the wrong direction when you step into the street!'

'So I'll die happy,' he snorted. 'Keep a watch out of the window.'

'For what?'

'For that fat little private eye who followed us yesterday. I spotted him just a minute ago.'

'That enquiry agent? And if I see him?'

'Dear God, make up your mind,' he muttered. 'If your family came from Chicago, talk like a Chicagoan. Never mind all this limey business. Her Majesty's postal service! Enquiry agents! Indeed!'

'Don't be a bully,' she snapped, drawing herself up to her full height and glaring at him. 'I'm as American as you are. I just *happen* to have lived in the Grenadines for some time! Can I help it if my father was footloose?'

'No, I don't suppose so.' He sighed. 'I'm going to send a cable message overseas,' he explained as he searched his pockets for the right credit card. 'If you see him, come running after me. Especially if he comes into the bank.'

Peggy shook her head sadly. 'It must be the heat,' she said soothingly. 'I know I forgot to tell you to wear a hat when you're out in the sun. This is the bank, Mr Marston. If you want to send a cablegram you go over to the post office.'

He grinned down at her. 'You've a lot to learn, little Miss Mitchell,' he announced grandly. 'If I were to walk into the post office the people watching us would know we were sending a message, and I'm sure that, with enough money for grease, they could find someone to tell them what my message said. But when we go into the bank, they'll expect us to do something about banking, and maybe they won't bother to enquire too closely. And, in the meantime, every bank maintains a cable service of its own.'

'Which they'll never share with you,' she announced in an injured tone of voice. 'Banks are great about not doing things for you until you can prove you don't need them!'

'Banks are always very friendly to people who deposit a large letter of credit,' he chuckled. 'They fall all over themselves when the numbers go over fifty thousand dollars. Sending a cablegram for me would be nothing. Probably the manager would also be happy to shine my shoes. Just watch, missy.'

She watched him go, striding across the polished floor like some predatory beast. The set of his shoulders, the trim swing of his narrow hips—for some reason she could not understand these simple things caught at her mind and held her. But—'Watch out of the window,' he had commanded, and she shivered to think how easily she had disobeyed. The window was at her back. She whirled around and looked out into the sunny, crowded street.

And there he was, the little fat man, leaning against the corner of the shopping mart across the street, dressed in an off-white shirt and trousers that curved over his ample stomach, held in place by red braces. His face ran red with perspiration, and he kept jiggling the suit-jacket draped over one arm so that he could wipe his forehead with a huge handkerchief. He looked as out of place as a chicken at a fox convention!

'Jim,' she whispered. 'He's here!' She gave herself a good shake as she realised what she was doing. Pragmatic, practical Margarita, she told herself sarcastically, echoing her father's often-repeated little chant. What the devil has happened to you in the last few days? You've come apart at the seams! Where the devil is that man?

The officials of the bank were scattered throughout the building in little cubicles set off from each other by glass-panelled walls. She could see a few customers scattered here and there; none of them was Jim Marston. Peggy scuttled down the row of compartments, peering into each one in turn until she found him. He was leaning over the desk of a vice-president, filling in a message from the code-book he carried in his pocket. He stopped to ponder a couple of times, pencilled a few notes in the book, and then laughingly exchanged a few words with the bank official. 'Yes, we would be happy to send your message,' the vice-president assured him. 'And with maximum confidentiality.'

Peggy studied his profile. Examined it in microscopic detail, in fact. His hair was loose and silky, cut just above his collar, with a little cowlick in front that continually threatened to fall into his eyes. His forehead was broad, unlined, and deeply tanned. He had a nose fit for an emperor. Not too big, just commanding. It widely separated those two deep hazel eyes, which seemed to gleam as he laughed. There was a dimple on his near cheek, and a slightly determined cleft in his chin. He looked like the winner in an 'I am Important' contest. She became so engrossed in her study that he startled her when he touched her button nose with a finger and said, 'Daydreaming?'

She jumped backwards an inch or two. 'I was just— waiting for you to get finished,' she stammered.

Those eyes gleamed at her. 'Which I did—oh—some ten minutes ago,' he chuckled. 'See something you like?'

'I was——' She stopped dead in her tracks to think things out. 'It *couldn't* have been ten minutes ago,' she stated firmly after a moment, and blushed as his grin widened.

'I don't mind if you just came to admire,' he prompted.

'But I didn't. He's here,' she babbled. 'He's standing across the street with red braces and he's watching the door and I——'

'Whoa!' he commanded. 'Catch your breath!'

Peggy could feel anger building higher and higher. In just thirty seconds more she fully intended to do him some damage. 'Don't treat me like your idiot child,' she muttered, tilting her sharp fingernails up in a clawlike gesture. Jim Marston put up both hands in a boxer's protective pose. The bank official cleared his throat officiously.

'Hey!' Count ten, she told herself, gritting her teeth. Count twenty. He's come to fix my problems. God knows I can't fix them for myself! Take deep breaths. Count to twenty again! Fix my problems? I wonder if he's really a fixer, or only a con man? Five, four, three, two, and one!

'The detective is across the street,' she stated flatly, enunciating each word carefully.

'Very good.' Jim took her elbow and began to guide her out of the building. 'Now,' he ordered as they neared the door, 'we need full acting ability. You love me madly. Take my arm, it looks better that way. Look dependent. There's the girl. Watch it!'

'Well, I can't look at you forever without stumbling on this pavement.' The words were hissed at him between smiling teeth.

'Think positive,' he insisted. 'Now I put the arm around you, and you put yours around my waist——!'

'It won't fit,' she muttered, still smiling. 'Too much waist.'

'Too little arm.' He grinned down at her, and for just a second a frog blocked her throat and her heart skipped a beat.

They went through the graceless warehouse district at a casual walk, until finally they were out on the pierside, and the lovely harbour lay before them. The water seemed as calm as glass. Not a ripple of wind stirred. But just south of them the regular freighter of the Geest Line was loading bananas for Britain. A ragged line of longshoremen, each carrying on his shoulder a stem of bananas wrapped in plastic, was trotting into the open ship's hold.

'All the way to England,' she explained when he questioned her. 'Can I stop looking adoring now?'

'No,' he commanded, 'but you could explain what's going on. What I know about bananas could be written on the back of a postage stamp.'

'Well.' She stopped to clear the huskiness from her throat. 'Bananas are now our major crop. Most of them go to Britain. The stems are wrapped in the plastic bags while still on the trees, after they've been sprayed.'

'Sprayed?' he muttered. 'Slow down. The detective is having trouble keeping up.'

'Yes, sprayed,' she insisted. 'They're sprayed against bugs, sprayed to keep them from ripening—lord, if the people in England ever tasted a real tree-ripened banana they'd be totally shocked. But then, there has to be *some* way to deliver the fruit before it spoils, and the spraying evidently doesn't detract a *great deal* from the flavour. There he is now, ducking behind that truck. What next, Mr Sherlock Holmes?'

'Now we wander down to my yacht,' he chuckled. 'Aimlessly. Keep adoring, lady.'

'My teeth hurt from all this smiling,' she grumbled. 'All right, I'm adoring! Don't push! And don't squeeze, either! I'm like a hand of bananas. You squeeze too hard and I pop out of my skin!'

'Hand?' he asked. 'Is there a separate language for bananas?'

'Of course not,' she grumbled through wide smiling teeth. 'Just a few names. A single banana is known as a finger. A cluster of bananas is a hand. A dozen hands or more make up a stem. Where's your yacht?'

'Moored down there at the end,' he told her. 'You can stop adoring now. He stopped back there once we started out on to the pier.'

'Well thank the lord for that,' Peggy said solemnly as she closed her mouth and wiggled her jaw back and forth to relieve the strain. He brought her to a stop beside a beautiful, white-hulled sailing sloop, some forty feet in length, gaff-rigged, its mahogany deck gleaming from a fresh scrubbing, all its brass fittings polished to a sun-echo, its sails furled and covered, and a proud ensign flying at the stern.

'Meet the *Sea-Witch*.' He offered her a hand to step over the combing into the cockpit where, sea-wise, she slipped out of her high-heeled shoes to keep from scarring the finish. He noticed out of the corner of his eye and gave her full marks. In fact, he told himself, there's little this lady can't master. And the more I see *of* her, the more of her I'd like to see! In the classic Yankee sense, she'd make a great bowsprit!

'What do I do now?' Her warm, clear voice was another point in her favour. And I'd really like to tell her, he thought. Something on the order of 'lie down here, I want to talk to you'! But his rational mind chided him. It was not a question of will she or won't she. It was just that now was just not the time, nor here the place.

'Why don't you just relax?' he advised her. 'We need to waste some time to allow the little man to make his report. And then I have to make a couple of telephone calls to New York.'

'But you did that last night,' Peggy reminded him. 'You talked long enough to double the national debt. And if you had anything more to say you could have gone over to the post office.' She settled on to the cushioned bench that half-circled the cockpit. 'I'd say I don't understand you, but you'd think there was an echo in the place.'

'I can see you don't know much about worldwide sales techniques,' he laughed. 'You don't watch enough television.' She glared at him. There was no electricity on the Mitchell plantation, and no television either. 'Now'— he latched on to her hand and pulled her closer—'comes the explanation.'

Peggy looked at him with a wild gleam in her eyes. Surely now the men in the white coats and the big butterfly nets would come for him? He seemed to read her mind—at least, so the big grin indicated.

'What we did in the bank,' he continued, 'was to send a coded message to my office, telling them what I want them to do. Included in that message were instructions to forget about the radio-telephone call I'm about to make. Got it?'

'Not a bit,' she sighed. 'Why are you going to make a radio-telephone call now that you want them to forget about?'

'Because, love, every boat in the harbour can listen in on this call I'm about to make. I'm about to tell a big lie, and I want our friendly followers out there to hear all about it. In words of one syllable, missy, I'm about to bait a trap. Now what do you think?'

'I have the terrible feeling that I'm going to wind up in gaol,' she sighed. 'And the gaols on this island are not very—comfortable. And Bea will be angry enough to bite my head off, and if my brother Andrew ever hears about this, I'll *really* be in the soup. That's what I think. I thought we were engaged in a perfectly legitimate business deal. Now it's sounding more and more like a conspiracy. I wish I were sure about you, Jim Marston.'

'Hey, come on now.' He squeezed the hand he was holding very gently. 'This is all a very legitimate operation. Nobody's going to gaol. All my people are beating the woods for customers to buy arrowroot. It will be a simple business deal, just as I explained to you yesterday.'

'I think you'll have to excuse my ignorance,' she returned in that soft murmur that made him perk up his ears. 'The rest of my family is very intelligent, but when brains were handed out I must have been standing behind the door. I guess maybe if I were a little older——'

'How old are you?' he interrupted gruffly.

'Twenty-six.'

'You're joking! Twenty-six? You hardly look seventeen!'

'Well, I am,' she assured him, and then picked up the thread of her conversation. 'Because I was the only girl, and we moved around so much, I didn't have the chance for elementary and secondary schooling. Mother tutored me, in between chores, and I read a great deal. My mother was once a nurse, you know. That may be what urged me to go to nursing school.'

'No, I didn't know,' he corrected. 'So that's why you're so quick with diagnoses. I suspect you learned a great deal from your tutor.'

'Maybe,' she sighed, 'but reading the encyclopaedia doesn't make up for actually experiencing the Great Works.'

'Now you're going to tell me you read the encyclopaedia from cover to cover?'

'You needn't be sarcastic, Mr Marston,' she said in a condemning voice. 'I wasn't going to tell you any such thing, but now that you bring it up, that's just what I did. Three times, the 1946 edition. And I read the Bible from cover to cover six times. Would you like some applicable quotes?'

He could feel the sting behind the words. They dug into his conscience and rattled around in his mind. Superior Jim Marston, he castigated himself. No bigger snob was ever born, James, than yourself. This poor kid—correction—this poor woman has probably been through a thousand things you never could dream of, and here you are talking down to her as if she were some backwoods bimbo! And yet, like any man, he felt the need to defend himself.

'Jesus wept,' he offered. She sniffed at him, which is just what I deserve, he told himself. And then, lamely, 'Well, it's the best I could dredge up at a moment's notice.'

Her little button nose went up another notch. 'I could recite from the Song of Solomon,' he offered tentatively. She shook her head sadly.

'You don't have to defend *your* education,' she advised him gently. 'The Good Book says that "the wicked flee when no man pursueth".' And with that liberal application of sarcasm she turned her lovely back and completely ignored him!

And that, he told himself, takes care of you, Jim Marston. Zap! The only thing left for you to do is to take refuge in chauvinism. Like, wouldn't she look great stretched out naked on your black silk sheets? With all that flaming red hair, and that big smile, and those big— oh, wow! The thought cheered him as he went down into the day cabin and switched on the radio equipment.

Peggy watched him without moving. There had been no invitation. Perhaps the cabin was too small for the pair of them? Casually she slipped off her big straw hat and moved to the hatchway to peer down. There was more than sufficient room down there. Room enough for an orgy! She blushed as the words took on meaning, and her green eyes sparkled in the sunlight. I wonder what he really thinks of me? she asked herself, and shrugged her shoulders, discouraged. There was no way to tell. Lorelei? Combing my hair at the bend of the river, luring sailors to—whatever it was that Lorelei lured people to? Her innate sense of humour caught her up. If that's what he thinks!

She perched herself on the portside rail, tossed her hat across the cockpit to the other side, and let the sea breezes ruffle her hair. The little comb in her handbag would hardly suit but it would serve as a prop for this Caribbean Lorelei. Still smiling, she leaned back against a halyard and began to comb while she listened.

'Hello, Larry?' The radio spoke back to him, metallic and muffled and unintelligible. 'Yes,' he said. 'This is phase two. Now this conversation is confidential, you understand, and the subject is arrowroot, got it?'

Again the radio muttered at him. 'That's right,' he laughed. 'Look, this could be a quick sell and a big turnover. Check again with your sources, about using arrowroot as the stiffener in quality computer paper—you know. We can promise a one-time sale, and guarantees for future production that'll get the unions off their back. Get them tied up hand and foot in a long-term futures contract. Got it?'

A pregnant silence, and then he continued, 'Yes. There's only one good source here on the island now. Everyone else has gone out of business.' And at that point he must have closed a hatch, for she heard nothing more of the long conversation.

The radio squawked back at him, and suddenly the Kingstown operator came on, loud and clear, with time and charges. In a moment Jim Marston came back up on deck, laughing.

'What's so funny,' she asked grumpily. What she had heard had seemed pretty innocuous, but what about the part she hadn't heard? But when he came over and sat beside her, thigh touching thigh casually, Peg Mitchell had the sudden feeling that her body was trying to tell her something important! A fog developed in her mind, obscuring all her righteous anger, her careful logic. The corners of her mouth, which had been turned down in a frown that made her square face seem so ordinary, now tilted upwards, and her dimples developed. An on-shore breeze was rising, snatching at her fire-red hair, tossing it in more than usual confusion. He moved in closer to the source, to stifle the silky cloud.

One of his arms came round her shoulders to help support himself. For a glorious moment she revelled in all the feelings within her. For just a moment, until Bea's face appeared in her mind. No words, just that loving black face, warning. 'I'm—sorry,' she stammered as she wiggled away from him and stood up. 'I didn't mean to——'

'Well, I did,' he chuckled, 'but obviously it's not on. Have you seen anything more of that sneak?'

'I'm not sure,' she said. Her voice quavered; she hurried to the other side of the deck and took a deep breath. 'I—think he boarded that red yacht at the other side of the dock. But——'

'Go ahead,' he told her as she hesitated. 'What's going on?'

'Yes,' she said. 'What's going on? I don't understand you, Mr Marston—er—Jim. Sometimes I get the feeling that you're the biggest confidence-man in the western hemisphere. Uncaught, that is.' He almost broke up laughing.

Well, she told herself, he does have a funny-bone, but I didn't say anything all *that* funny. 'Mr Marston?'

'Wait a minute,' he gasped, holding his stomach as if it pained him. 'The greatest con-man still at large, huh?' He was still laughing, in a deep rumble that shook him. 'Well, I hate to disappoint you, little lady. I'm just a prosaic businessman.'

'I don't know just how you mean that,' she said seriously. 'There are a great many businessmen in gaol these days—and apparently a great many con-men still free. I hope—you're not going to get me mixed up in something illegal, are you?'

He stood up and stretched, almost to the sky, she thought, and a couple of steps brought him over in front of her. His big hands cradled her chin and tilted it up. 'No, we're not going to do anything illegal,' he assured her. Her neck ached from looking upward; she struggled to her feet. The movement brought her all the closer to him. A closeness that frightened her. Her mind sent orders; her body refused to move.

His hands moved to her shoulders. 'There are two things that make the business world go round,' he said softly. 'Ambition and greed. All we're doing is offering some ambitious people a chance to satisfy their greed.'

'I don't understand,' she sighed, slumping against him. His arms came around her as she relaxed, emphasising the comfort.

'I've set everything in motion,' he told her. 'Tomorrow there's something I want you to do for me, and then you'll go home. In a few days I think I'll be able to turn up a buyer. If so, these people will come to you, Peggy, and eagerly make you an offer for your arrowroot.' He named a figure that made her head spin. She stiffened, but his arms held her close, and in a second she relaxed again.

'You will, equally innocently, insist that they meet your figure, and that they buy the crop in the ground.'

'But——'

'Hush,' he chuckled. 'It's only a business deal. I want you to make a good profit, because you'll owe me a nominal fee, right?' When he said it like that, it *did* sound reasonable. She nodded agreement.

'As I said, they'll buy it in the ground,' he continued. 'At which point you will insist that Henry and the villagers be hired to harvest the crop. And incidentally, Miss Mitchell, you will insist on payment in cash, or a certified cheque. In deals like this you have to pin the buyer down.'

'Well, thank you for the lecture,' she returned, pulling out of his arms. 'I'm going to be sure to write that down for my brother. Andrew will undoubtedly find it of great use when he takes over the farm.'

'Oh, lord,' he sighed. 'Can't you just trust me? Well, I'm finished here. Let's get back to the hotel, lovely lady.'

'I wish you wouldn't be so free with titles,' she suggested as she took his hand and was assisted out of the cockpit and on to the pier. 'Lovely lady, indeed! It confuses a girl like me. You know, by the way, that it's going to rain?'

He pulled her to a stop and turned full circle to examine the clouds. Black, angry clouds, boiling up from the south-west. 'I meant to ask you about that,' he told her as he took her elbow and urged her forward. She balked. Puzzled, he frowned down at her. 'It *is* going to rain,' he insisted. 'Hard.'

'I know that,' she chided him. 'I'm the one who lives here. Remember? This is the rainy season.'

'But nobody wears a raincoat or carries an umbrella?'

'Of course not. Things are arranged much more satisfactorily around here than up in New York. It rains every day at four o'clock. Sensible people plan their day so they can pop in somewhere at that time. Late tea, or a pub, or a browsing store, that sort of thing.'

'Then I suggest we run like hell,' he snorted. 'According to my watch it's ten past four.'

'No matter where we headed, we couldn't make it,' she assured him in the voice that teachers reserved for backward pupils. 'Back to the boat, Mr Marston, and batten down the hatches. I'll make you a cuppa.'

He grinned down at her and wheeled around, no longer urging, but almost towing her behind him. Her tiny legs were moving at flank speed, while he appeared to be barely strolling. 'For your information,' he said with a laugh as he lifted her clear of the rail and almost dropped her into the cockpit, 'I don't have any hatches to batten on this boat. Watch your noggin.' One of his big hands pushed her head down as she clattered down the short companionway into the day cabin. She landed on the lower deck askew, and wavered across the narrow passage, trying to regain her balance. Behind her, he slid the covers closed just as the tropical rain began to hurl huge drops at them.

The boat rocked for a moment, pitched a couple of times, and then settled down. The sound of the deluge on the roof was almost deafening. 'Lucky!' she shouted at him. 'Where do you keep things?'

'I'll get it,' he yelled back. 'Take a chair.'

There was no chair to be had, but a tiny table, well-fastened, took up half the space, and on the far side of it was a cushioned bench. Peggy grabbed at a bulkhead to steady herself, and slid into the bench as gracefully as possible. Jim busied himself at the little galley set against the hull opposite the table. A small primus stove, some storage areas, and a set of unbreakable china made up the total. As in everything he did, he seemed so efficient! She stared hungrily at him as he worked, wondering why. True, there had not been *many* men in her life, but there had been enough to teach her the basics of man-watching. So why am I acting like a teenager on her first crush? she asked herself. And found no answer.

He was back with two steaming cups as she managed to smooth down her dress and give her hair a haphazard brushing.

'I like your hair better when it's more casual,' he complained as he grounded the two mugs on the table. 'It has almost the same colouring as my eldest niece's. She calls it ridiculous! Do you take milk and sugar?'

'Well, I don't—like it loose, that is,' she snapped, defensively embarrassed by her thoughts. 'It makes me look like a child! No milk, no sugar.'

'Everyone to his own tastes,' he murmured. 'What's set you off this time?'

'I don't know what you mean.' She snatched up the hot mug, ignored its temperature, and sipped. 'Dear God!' she grumbled as she set it down. 'I thought it was——'

'Coffee,' he chuckled. 'The real American drink!'

'I thought it was tea,' she almost shouted at him. 'That's what people drink on St Vincent! Tea. That's what a cuppa is!'

He shrugged his shoulders and grinned. 'So I messed up again. Beat me around the head and shoulders. Or should I kneel down and cry *mea culpa*?'

Her glare might well have melted his head from his shoulders, but that grin was too much for her. She felt her lips trembling at the corners, and, unable to control her face, gave it all up in a lovely smile. 'I'm sorry,' she apologised. 'I keep forgetting that we speak different languages, both called English. No, all you need do is pass me the milk, and a lot of sugar.'

He complied, the grin fading from his face, replaced by a solemn concern. The table jiggled as he squeezed in behind it, barely inches from her. Unconsciously she shifted away. 'I've been nothing but trouble for you, Peggy, haven't I?' She shook her head to deny it.

'No, really,' he insisted gruffly. 'From the moment we met, I've given you nothing but trouble.' He cupped his hands around his own mug, as if drawing strength from its heat. 'And to tell the truth,' he continued, 'I don't understand you either, missy. May I call you that?'

'Of course,' she agreed readily. 'All my family do. I guess I'm not much different from the majority of women you know, am I?'

He sipped at his coffee, considering. 'I've known a great many different kinds of women,' he admitted. 'Some had aspects of your—strengths. Nobody had everything. Any woman who has managed a plantation for the length of time you have I respect. And the compassion you have for your family and your folk: I like that, too. Everyone I meet seems to know you—and like you. And yet, knowing all that, *I* don't know *you* at all, do I? The real you?'

'It's hard to see inside a person,' she responded softly. 'I guess that doesn't happen—except when you really love someone. Or you are loved by someone. I'm sure when you were a child——'

'That horse won't run,' he interrupted. 'My father was a gambler. On the stock market, I grant you. They didn't call him "gambler". But that's what he was. And he was sick with it, as if he had a disease. Nothing would do for him except winning! He made millions; he lost millions. Between bouts he lost his family. My father considered that we children were nothing more than an aggravating nuisance. So he shut us out of what little life we had shared. When I was eighteen I wanted to go to college, so I approached him. Instead of agreeing, he gave me four million dollars and told me to get out of his life!'

Peggy shook her head in sympathy, laid her hand over his on the table and gently squeezed. He looked up at her and one corner of his mouth turned up in a sort of smile.

'So you went off to college?' she prompted.

'No, lord, no,' he chuckled grimly. 'No, indeed. I was my father's son. The only acceptable goal was winning. So I took my four-million-dollar birthright and followed him into the stock market. We fenced with each other and a thousand others daily, but he never ever spoke a word directly to me again. Five years' worth of silence, can you imagine that?'

'No, I can't imagine that,' she sighed. 'I had troubles with my father, but none like yours. Were you two ever reconciled?'

He laughed abruptly, a barking noise that contained no humour. 'Reconciled? Never. I had a chance to make a great killing a couple of years ago. A real corporate raid. Piracy. At least, I thought it was. As it turned out, the people with whom I was working were setting up a scam, an insider trading deal, in which I was just part of the bait. I almost lost my shirt. By the four o'clock closing on the stock market that day the stock we were manipulating fell through the floor.'

He stopped to take another sip of the now luke-warm coffee. 'I managed to break even. My partners made a fortune.' He shook his head at the remembrance. 'A dozen or more other investors lost their shirts. I didn't know beforehand, but my father was the major loser.'

He stopped at that point, and there was a momentary silence while the rain hammered on the deck over their heads.

'I'm sure that's not the end of the story,' she prompted. 'Get it all out. It will do you good.'

'Will it?' he asked bleakly. 'So now you're a psychiatrist, too?'

'No,' she said quietly, patting the hand under hers. 'No. I'm just a human being willing to listen.'

He gritted his teeth, and she could see something gleaming in his hazel eyes. 'I should have been religious, so I could confess and be forgiven,' he muttered. 'But I'm not. You want to listen? Well, listen! The next morning I went to my father's house. I wanted to tell him how successful I had been—set up to be a real loser, but managing to win. Nobody answered the door, so I walked in. My father was sitting at his desk in the study, with a gun in his hand—some time during the night he had blown his brains out!'

'Oh, my God,' Peggy murmured, reaching for him to comfort. He snarled at her as he smashed his coffee-mug and got up.

'So now you know what makes James Marston run,' he muttered. 'I've spent years getting even with those—with my former partners. Now, I hope you're satisfied?' Peg hurried, but getting out from behind the table was a problem. Before she was free of it, Jim Marston had slammed his way out of the cabin, out into the tropical downpour. She stood at the foot of the companionway, dithering, with the rain blowing in her face.

How do you comfort a man who thinks he murdered his father? she asked herself, and found no answer in her own narrow experience. But there was an intuitive knowledge, borne perhaps in the genes. She plucked up her courage and followed him out on to the open deck.

The wind was picking up, sending the huge raindrops almost sideways. Jim had gone forward, and was standing at the bow of the *Sea-Witch*, looking out into the harbour, one hand on the forward stays to maintain his balance. The distance between them could hardly be forty rainswept feet, but it looked like a thousand dangerous miles. Cautiously Peggy sidled around the projection that was the cabin roof, grasping for any support she could find. The rain had already soaked her to the skin. Her hair hung down like a wet mop. She could feel the rivulet of water running down her neck and between her breasts; the deck was slippery under her feet.

Jim turned around at that moment, alerted by the little squeak she had emitted when her foot slipped. 'Go back,' he yelled. 'You'll get soaked out here!'

'Sure I will,' she roared back at him, and then abandoned her safety-clutch at one of the bronze cleats on the mast and dashed straight out across the deck in his direction.

If he hadn't been watching, hadn't reached out one huge hand and caught her, she would undoubtedly have gone straight off the bow into the bay. But he was, and he did.

'You are probably the craziest woman I've ever known,' he grumbled as he folded her soaked form into his soaked chest. Luckily, as with most tropical rains, the water was warm. She snuggled herself as close as she could, using both hands around his waist to sustain herself, wriggling to get as close as any two people could be.

'Probably you're right,' she agreed. There was still a little squeak in her normally smooth contralto, a squeak of relief, or more likely of fright. They hugged each other tightly.

'I didn't mean to tell you all that garbage,' he said gruffly. 'I've never told anyone else, why would I tell you?'

She heard the words but could not summon an answer. It all seemed too clear to her. Peggy relaxed into a dreamy condition that let words and rain pass right over her, while thoughts and hopes ran wild.

'Why?' he insisted.

She shook herself out of her dream-state, hating to do so. The dream itself was already gone, and she could not remember even a tiny part of it. Only that it was pleasant—most pleasant. And he had been in it.

'Because you just needed to tell somebody,' she said firmly, and squeezed tighter.

'Hmmph,' was all he replied. They stood there, interlocked, looking to the west. The far edge of the rain-cloud was in sight, and beams of sunlight were breaking through holes in the clouds, sending down little pillars of light that seemed to pierce the tossing ocean and settle it. Gradually, as they watched, the far edge of the storm moved nearer, the sun moved lower, and it sparkled rainbows at them.

'Jim?'

'What?'

'You didn't kill your father, you know.'

'Maybe I know that,' he said softly. 'But I surely wasn't much help to him, was I?'

# CHAPTER FIVE

THEY came into the hotel dining-room at the stroke of noon on Sunday. 'Lord, my feet hurt,' Peggy grimaced as she took Jim's arm and followed the head waiter to a table in the far corner. The floor-to-ceiling windows were all open, and the breeze that came in off the ocean was laden with the scent of bougainvillaea.

'But it was all worth it, wasn't it?' Jim asked as he held her chair. 'Although I don't think I would want to do another botanical garden any time soon. You're sure it was Captain Bligh who brought those breadfruit trees?'

'Certain sure,' she returned, smiling. 'And St Mary's, the Catholic cathedral, was designed by a Belgian parish priest who remembered what European Gothic churches looked like. And no, I don't remember who designed and built Wesleyan Hall. You can't have everything, you know.'

'Well, we've arrived at *almost* everything,' he said jovially. 'My feet hurt too, and I think we've seen everything there is to be seen in Kingstown, haven't we?' And all the time he was talking he was manoeuvring her carefully so she might not see the group almost hidden in the far corner behind the potted plants. Vera Helst, of course, and a couple of compatriots. So she's abandoned the detective and brought in help from the mainland, he thought. A lawyer, for sure, and perhaps a senior member of the firm? He rubbed his hands gleefully. The fish were taking the bait. This sting might be one of the finest in his repertoire!

'Why are you so suddenly jovial?' Peg asked as she sat down and looked around.

'Because it's a fine day, and I've been seen around and about with the most beautiful woman on the island.'

'You need to have your eyes examined,' she retorted.

'Maybe I do. Where the devil is the menu?'

'It's Sunday afternoon,' she informed him, with a touch of provincialism in her voice. 'The tourists are either eating out or packing up. The hotel only has one item on Sunday. Rack of lamb, mint sauce, sweet potato, and possibly a salad.'

'Maybe we should have gone to McDonald's,' he grumbled. 'Where do they get all that outlandish stuff?'

'All home-grown,' she grinned. 'Mesopotamia Valley grows everything a British heart could desire. So do we. Hello, Joseph.' She looked up to give a greeting to the waiter who had ambled over to them. 'Joseph is Henry's son,' she explained to Jim as an aside.

'I remember,' Marston said softly. 'Henry, the blacksmith!'

'Missy Mitchell,' the waiter acknowledged. 'You know somethin' funny?'

'No, what, Joseph?'

'That lady over there, she done give me ten dollars to tell your name. Don' you think that's funny?'

'Which woman was that?' Peg asked, her curiosity piqued. She half rose in her chair to look around.

'It can't be anyone important,' Jim interrupted. 'I'll give you another ten if you make sure they find out where Miss Mitchell lives, after the fight!'

'Fight? There gonna be a fight?' the young man asked, his eyes lighting up with interest. 'Not on Sunday, there can't be no fight. Not here! Maybe in New York, OK. Maybe in London, OK, but not here in Kingstown!

Course, they ain't nothin' else goin' on here of a Sunday afternoon, either, unless you likes cockfights?'

'It won't be all that bad,' Jim assured him. An American ten-dollar bill seemed to walk across the table and disappear into Joseph's hand. 'We'll have the special.'

'Comin' as fast I can walk,' the young waiter promised. And kept his promise.

'What in the world are you talking about?' Peg snapped. 'What woman? What fight? And why my address?'

'Just one of my little habits,' Jim responded. 'I hate to see so much peace and quiet. Can hardly stand the stuff, to tell the truth. Have confidence in me, Peggy. Trust me.'

'Oh, sure,' she murmured as she attacked the lamb. 'Trust me. That's what my father always used to say.' Which was enough to turn off the conversation for the rest of the meal.

'That's the best service I've had in years,' Jim said appreciatively, as he watched the ruin of the rack of lamb being whisked away, to be followed by cheese and gâteau. 'Now, are you ready to go?'

'Hey, I don't get dessert very often,' she complained. 'Surely I can finish this?'

'So finish,' he grumbled. 'But we don't wait for the coffee. That would spoil the scene.' He had both forearms on the table, leaning across the narrow space between them. Peggy watched him carefully. This was a different Jim Marston. The first had been the battered charmer with roving hands, the second the passionately bitter man who spoke about his father and stood on the bow of the boat with her in the rain; and this one—well, definitely the hunter. Poised as if on a hair-trigger, waiting to go into action. Waiting to bite somebody's head off, she told herself. And I'm glad it isn't mine! A delicious warmth swept through her. She fumbled in her own mind, unable to put a name to the feeling. There was something about Jim—regardless of all her doubts—that she liked!

'Now,' he commanded softly. She dropped her spoon. He took her left hand in both of his, leaned even farther across the table with a glare on his face. 'I want you to do the most stupid thing in the world, Peggy. I want everyone who watches us to think I've just made you a proposition that you don't like.' His fingers squeezed her hand until it hurt.

'Why—why should I do something like that?' she asked. 'You're hurting me, Jim! Turn me loose!'

'That's it,' he muttered. 'Look terrified.' She didn't have to put on an act, she *was* terrified. He pulled her up out of her chair. She fought back, but his grip was too strong. And all the time he was whispering instructions. 'There's a taxi waiting for you outside at the kerb, already paid for. Now, when I release your wrist, slap my face and run. Get in the cab. I'll get in touch with you later tonight. Got it?'

'No, I don't have it,' she wailed. 'Why are you doing this? Let me go!'

'Yeah,' he murmured. 'Good show. Don't forget, the cab's right outside the door. Now, hit me.' His hand fell away from her wrist. Everyone in the room was watching. 'Hit me,' he repeated. Confused, irritated, she glared at him. 'Hit me,' he repeated again. 'Come on!'

'I'll come on,' she snarled at him, and swung at him. But instead of delivering the open-palm slap he evidently expected, she doubled up her fist and slammed it into his altogether too arrogant nose.

Peggy Mitchell had never doubted her punching ability, but this was absurd. His nose seemed to blossom and drip red, his heavy body went backwards over the chair and on to the adjacent table. The table collapsed, split down the middle. Jim Marston, wrapped in the tablecloth, fell with the wreckage and lay there.

A dozen knives and forks at other tables paused in mid-air. Jim Marston lay quietly in the middle of the debris. Peggy, completely confused, jumped back out of the way, knocking her own chair back in the doing, and ran for the door. The little centre of fear in the back of her mind had spread its tentacles throughout her body. As her adrenalin pumped, so did her feet. Out of the double doors of the restaurant, through the somnolent lobby, down the three stone steps that led to the street, and in through the open door of the taxi.

'Out of the city, quickly!' she gasped as she struggled to sit back in the seat.

'I know the place,' the placid driver assured her. He snapped her door shut, revved the engine, and zoomed round the square towards the highway. Crouched in the taxi, she watched through the back window as Jim Marston appeared on the steps of the hotel, waving one arm in the air and using the other to hold a towel to his red-stained nose. He yelled something at her that she definitely did not want to hear! She huddled down in the back seat. 'Go faster,' she yelled.

Nightfall. A strong wind was whistling through the thick forests that held sway on the mountainside. Only the one lamp in the kitchen lit the house. Bea and Peggy sat on the porch, protected by the mosquito screens, rocking.

'An' you say he's coming?' Bea leaned forwards to watch Peggy's face.

'He said he was,' the girl repeated dully. 'I don't believe him. I never hit anybody as hard as that, not in my whole life. I don't even understand why he—why he asked me to. I think he's gone back to his boat and is probably a hundred miles away from St Vincent by now! Damn! He's a good man, Bea, but I just don't understand what's going on!'

'Sure he is,' the old housekeeper agreed. 'All men, they good people up until they get what they want, huh? He behave heself?'

'A perfect gentleman,' Peggy sighed. And it was her own sigh that bothered her. What did you want of him, she asked herself. That he *not* be so perfect? That he jump on you, or at least make a gesture? You can't have your cake and eat it too, Margarita. You're suffering from a bad case of the itch, aren't you? Tired of being so virtuous, yourself? Wondering what it's all about, this sex business?

'Well, you jus' see he stays that way,' Bea grumbled. 'I don't understand nothin' about this whole affair. An' the little bit I do understand I don't like. Tell me again. *He* gonna buy the arrowroot?'

'Not he,' Peggy repeated for the tenth time. 'This other group. They're going to buy it all—and for heaven's sake don't ask me why—because I really don't know myself!' Her voice rode the upward scale hysterically. It had all sounded so plausible when he had explained it, but now it was almost nine o'clock, and he hadn't come. What had seemed so simple had become complex. The sale had almost fallen from her mind. *He* had become more important than his business deal!

The old dog in the kennel behind the house barked once and then fell silent. 'Somebody comin',' Bea announced. She got up out of her rocking-chair, stretching her back against the arthritic pains creeping up on her, and leaned against the porch rail. 'Him, all right.'

'You can't know that,' Peggy railed, 'It's pitch dark out there.'

'I can tell. Him all right,' Bea repeated. And in a moment it *was* him, climbing the steps up to the porch, pushing against the squeak of the old screen door, stepping into the half-light from the kitchen.

Him, all right, Peggy told herself as she leaped to her feet. Run to him, her devils whispered. Hold hard, her subconscious mind dictated. Like a weathervane caught up in crosswinds, Peggy Mitchell froze in position, her hands balled up into fists clutched against her breasts, her feet shifting an inch or two, forwards and back.

'You,' she stammered, biting back the tears. And how about that, stupid? she lectured. When he does come you start to cry!

'What do you know?' he chuckled. 'It really is me. What a wonderful welcome!'

'Watch you lip, man,' Bea snapped. 'They's a lady present!'

'With *this* lady it's my nose I have to watch,' he replied. 'Man, what a left hook you have, Peggy. I'll have to remember that!'

'Bea, please.' Peggy was still fighting the desire to run to him, and losing. 'How did you get here, James?'

'A rental four-wheel-drive,' he told her as he closed the screen door behind him. 'I left it down in the village. The blacksmith gave me a hard time for a little bit, until I pulled a little rank on him.'

'Huh!' Bea snorted.

'I don't understand,' Peggy said. 'Rank? What rank?'

That big grin was back on his face. 'I told him Miz Bea was waiting for me,' he said. 'It was almost as if I had invoked the Queen's authority. They hid the car away for me, and provided a guide right up to the edge of the plateau. Now then, how about my welcome?' He stalked across the porch, ignoring Bea's glare, gathered Peggy up in his arms, and kissed her with a great deal of enthusiasm.

Bea was about to thunder down on his head when she noticed that the enthusiasm was not one-sided. At which point the housekeeper nodded her head. He wasn't *exactly* what she wanted for Missy—but good-looking men were scarce on the ground these days! So she let the proceedings proceed for another minute or two before she interrupted.

'Suppose you might be hungry?' Bea tapped him on the shoulder to be sure he knew he was the subject of the discussion. 'Got a nice bit of that roast shoulder left over.' He lifted his head, a dazed expression in his eyes. At the same time Bea swung her flat heavy hand and bounced it off Peggy's bottom. The girl, looking as dazed as he, bounced back to reality, blushed, and pushed away from him.

'Yes, of course,' Peggy stammered. 'You must be hungry. I'm—sorry. I forgot—I'm a terrible hostess.'

He looked at them both, still grinning. He had another idea in mind, but there was too much opposition for it at the moment. Somehow or other, right in the middle of that faked fight, the little lady had landed a knockout blow on his heart! 'Yeah,' he acknowledged. 'I surely am hungry.'

Peggy, recipient of a quick, quirky look, knew it wasn't pork he was hungry for, and blushed again. Bea, intent on steering the whole situation back to safer ground, grabbed at his arm and towed him off to the kitchen, where pork, sweet potato, and candied yams were the only conversation-starters allowed for the next thirty minutes.

'Ah, that was most satisfying,' he finally grunted as he laid down his fork and pushed his chair back. 'You're some wonderful cook, Miz Bea.'

'Not me,' the housekeeper interjected. 'Missy cooked it all. She a wonderful cook, that girl. And sews, and handles the chores—why, ain't many women her age can do what she do!'

'Bea, please!' Peggy begged. It had been her only line for most of the evening. Bea, please, and then a fiery red blush in embarrassment. You don't have to sell me off at the auction block, Bea, she whispered to herself. I don't think he wants me—well, maybe he does—but not for what I want. Dear lord in heaven, what's the matter with me?

'Don't you think so, Peggy?' His words buzzed around her head like mosquitoes, as they finally penetrated.

'Oh, yes,' she agreed hesitantly, not knowing to what she was agreeing.

'Nonsense!' Bea put her foot down hard. 'You not gonna go walkin' in the moonlight at this hour, just the two of you. No, sir! In case you ain't noticed, there ain't no moonlight. It's come to rain again.'

'I—yes, of course,' Peggy stammered, looking for a quick change in the conversation. 'I suppose—about the sale. It's off?'

'Everything's fine,' he confirmed. 'I think we can expect action in a very short time. This contact I made has gone back to her home office for approval, and it looks as if they'll be sending a couple of vice-presidents down to close the deal. I *think* that's what is going on, although I can't be sure. I don't remember when I've been knocked to the floor so jauntily.' He reached up and gently patted his nose. What an actor, Peggy told herself!

'You—missy? You knocked the man on his——'

'On the floor, Bea,' Peggy quickly interjected. 'On the floor. It was all part of a—game—we were playing.

Maybe I got too enthusiastic. I really didn't mean to——'

'Think nothing of it.' He chuckled. 'All is forgiven. I just didn't know that young ladies packed such a wallop. But anyway, after I chased you out the door and——'

'You chased her out the door!' Bea shouted.

'It was only a joke,' he reiterated hastily, backing away from the enraged housekeeper. 'Well, I went back to the bar for a little sympathy, and that's when I learned about the visiting vice-presidents. But there you go. Now, I've arranged with Henry, down in the village, to hold them up when they appear——'

'*If* they appear,' Peggy interrupted cautiously.

'When they appear,' he repeated. 'Some time in the next two or three days they will certainly come. I know very little about psychology, but a great deal about business, missy. They'll appear. And Henry will lead them around the barn a few times—just long enough to send us a warning. I'd be surprised if they're not here by tomorrow or the next day.'

'Can't be,' Bea said firmly. 'I gonna go see my sister. Can't have no visitors when just missy here.'

'And me,' Jim added. 'And me. I'm going to have to hide somewhere, but I'll be here, so don't worry.'

'I'm going to have so much help,' Peggy said, 'that I think I have to go to the bathroom. Excuse me.' The pair of them watched until she was out of sight.

'Huh,' Bea snorted. 'You bein' here, that worry me more than before, man. I—I dunno about you,' Bea said militantly. 'Sometimes I think nice, sometimes I think trouble. But I gonna find out, man. You sit there quiet. We gonna ask the cards.'

Jim settled back in his chair, shaking his head. 'Voodoo?'

'In Haiti they have voodoo,' Bea stated. 'Backward country. We British. You don't understand that, hey? We don't shake rattles, ask obeah man. But we do ask Tarot.' She reached behind her and brought out a large pack of playing cards. Not the regular cards, he noted, but of the same size and shape as a poker deck. Bea shuffled through the oversized pack, discarding more than half of them.

'We needs only the major arcana,' Bea said. 'Don't need no details. Tarot, Mr Marston. Nobody can lie to the cards, 'cause they read the heart, not the mind, huh? You don't believe?'

'Of course not,' he returned angrily. 'Mumbo-jumbo. There's no place in the jet-world for medieval mumbo-jumbo!'

'Good,' Bea shuffled the cards for a moment, a big grin shining on her face. 'You don't believe, the cards read you all the better. Shuffle for me.' She handed him the restricted pack. His hands moved automatically, with the residual skill of thousands of poker hands. When he slapped the cards down in front of her she pushed them into a fan-shape without turning them over. 'Choose,' she ordered.

'Mumbo-jumbo,' he repeated, but slipped a card out of the middle of the pack, turned it over, and dropped it on top of the pile. 'Make something out of that, lady.'

She grinned at him. 'I can make plenty, man,' she laughed, setting the card he had picked down in the middle of the table, with its orientation the same as when he had held it in his hand. 'This card is the Significator,' she droned. 'The death card. Notice. A skeleton knight, black armour, white horse. This is you today.'

'So I'm dead?' He laughed sarcastically.

'Not necessarily death of the body,' she chided him. 'The card means you have come to an end and a new beginning. You are dissatisfied with your life, and look to new, unknown things. There is an overtone of greed and unhappiness, man.'

He watched with a one-sided grin as Bea carefully picked up the pack, turned them so that she was oriented as he had been at the cutting. Mumbo-jumbo, he told himself. So she got lucky. Or overheard something I was saying somewhere. Bea took the first card from the top of the pack and laid it across the death card. 'The Hermit,' she announced. 'Notice he carries a lantern, looking.'

'For an honest man?' he chuckled. She grinned back at him.

'As you say. He looks for your future path, man. He looks for happiness. But this card lies negative. Which means he has to look inside himself. Maybe he looks for an honest man? Possible to find?'

Zap, he told himself, and squirmed nervously in his chair. So I've been honest—well, almost. Certainly, I've kept within the law, but is that being honest? Isn't that the question I've been asking myself all these months? But the old witch is just guessing, damn it!

Bea's fingers flipped the next card off the pack, being careful to turn it from side to side, never top to bottom. 'The Star,' she droned. 'This is the aura that surrounds you. Plenty. The woman pours from an inexhaustible spring, and everything is gold. You are surrounded by gold, man. No?'

'Not that I know of,' he said grimly. 'Holding of gold is prohibited to American citizens.' Bea looked up at him.

'That's what card says, too,' she told him. 'You live a good life, and are afraid to admit it. Outwardly you show sincerity; inward you show greed. You are not a bad man, but you think only of yourself. This you must change.'

'Oh, God,' he muttered, 'You talk like my mother. Always on my back.'

'Good woman,' Bea chortled. 'Maybe she reads Tarot, too. Now——' She flipped the next card over and placed it above the little pile she had been constructing. 'The Devil.' All joking disappeared from both their faces.

'Hanging over my head?' he asked pensively.

'Yes,' Bea said softly. 'Negative. It is also you. Card says you have powers; over money, love, people—you can control anything you want. You hold all powers. But you must be careful what you ask for, because you might get it!'

Because you might get it, he thought. And have to live with it the rest of your life, even though you don't really want it! As he pondered Bea went on, laying down the Wheel of Fortune to the left of the pile, but her words passed him by. Be careful what you ask for, he thought. Hell, I don't have a single idea for the future. Except for this little scam, or the lovely little lady that I'd like to try on for size. He snapped back to attention as Bea laid out four cards in a row, up the right-hand side of the pattern she was developing.

'These are the future,' she said as she tapped each one. 'The Tower. Of Babel, of course. Blackness, misery. Too much talking without understanding. You will make a wrong choice. There will be much danger. Physical danger to you and to someone important to you. There is travel—over water, I b'lieve. And fire and destruction. Very bad card, the Tower. But there is hope.' Her fingers tapped the next card. 'The Moon,' she said.

'What's that?' he asked solemnly, no longer chiding, no longer joking.

'The Moon,' she repeated. 'Everything in your mind is confusion. Nothing is what you think it is. You will have more evidence in time, and you will re-evaluate your life, and you will see everything in a better light. There is happiness when you come to enlightenment... And the Lovers.' Bea hurried on, as if anxious to see the end of the story. 'There will be love. There will be harmony between your inner and outer life.' She turned the next card over slowly, and a broad grin spread across her face.

'And this the last card,' she announced. 'We call it the World. Which means, out of love you will have all your heart's desires.' Peggy's footsteps could be heard coming down the hall. Bea scooped up all the cards, patted them fondly, and slipped them into the pocket of her apron.

Jim Marston was still facing her across the table, nibbling at his lip. 'And they lived happily ever after,' he sighed, and then shook himself out of the hypnosis. 'And I don't believe a damn word of it.'

'Of course not,' the housekeeper agreed. 'What modern man would? Only old superstition.'

'What superstition?' Peggy asked as she came into the room.

'Oh, nothing,' Jim replied. 'We were just commenting about all the superstitions that fill some of these islands!'

Peggy pulled up her chair and looked at them both. They were too serious for her own good, she thought. 'What is it, Bea? You're *not* going to see your sister tomorrow?'

'Oh, I gonna go,' the old woman returned with a smile. 'I think it over, and I gonna go. So long you two behave yourself!'

She got up, struggling with her arthritic knees, kissed Peggy's cheek, patted Jim on the head, and went to the door. 'And you, man. You remember what I say. Both hands in you pockets!'

'And whistle,' he chuckled as he turned to watch the housekeeper disappear down the hall.

Bea was up early the next morning. And because she was up, Peggy heard the noise and was up too. But it was a pair of crows squabbling outside his window that finally brought Jim Marston out, hair still dripping wet from the shower.

'I forgot the going-away,' he announced as he strolled into the kitchen. Peggy tried to slide into the background without too much success. She wanted to see what effect he had on Bea. It didn't take long to find out. The housekeeper cracked *four* of their precious eggs for him, and was scrambling them in butter—real butter! Actions speak louder than words?

'Good morning, Margaret.' He grinned down at her. Surely he knew just what I've been thinking, she thought. And the blush came. Along with a rising temper.

'Peggy,' she insisted. 'Or Margarita. There's nobody around here named Margaret!'

'Hush, missy,' Beau interrupted. 'Man only tryin' to be pleasant. Just 'cause you gets out of bed on the wrong side every morning don't mean the rest of us can't be pleasant.'

'I can be pleasant,' Peggy grumbled. 'And I don't get up *every* day in a grouch!' Nor do I get up every day with the need to defend myself, she thought as she looked up into those hazel eyes. So why today? Why should I *care* what this man thinks? Maybe we make a good pair: the slick New Yorker and the grouch? The idea caused the corner of her mouth to quiver. She ducked her head to hide the breakdown, her beautiful hair swinging across her face as an effective shield.

'Why don' you two walk me down to the bus and then go swimmin'?' Bea suggested as she worked on his breakfast at the stove.

'Swimming? I love swimming,' he volunteered. 'I didn't know you had a beach up at this end of the island.'

'Only a little thing, at the mouth of the river,' Peggy explained. 'About the only flat land we have in these parts.'

Bea grounded his breakfast plate in front of him, and he began to dig in. 'Yes,' he managed between mouthfuls, 'I'll be glad to accompany her.'

And how's that for a quick acceptance? Peggy thought. He gets it out even before the invitation! Did I *plan* to invite him? Did I plan to go swimming? Of course, the books are all posted, but I really should be helping out down in the truck gardens. But do I *want* to play truant and go off with him? That question added one more blush to the morning's activities. The answer was just too plainly yes! Helplessly she shrugged her shoulders and glared as that gleam sparkled in his eyes.

Three-quarters of an hour later, carrying a picnic basket in her arms, Peggy Mitchell strolled down the trail behind Bea. The housekeeper was dressed in her Sunday best, and Jim, carrying the battered suitcase filled with the housekeeper's vacation needs and a lunch basket, followed. The pair of them were carrying on an amiable discussion. About wind and rain and almonds and arrowroot and babies and—lord, the list was unending. And rather than be intimidated by it all, Jim Marston was more than holding his own. Peggy shook her head, and could not conceal the smile. Bea had his whole attention. And he hers.

All this on a day when Peggy Mitchell had selected her most ornate T-shirt to wear over the black one-piece swimsuit; had brushed her hair until it sparkled; had chosen her only crimson culottes; had added a touch of lipstick, a brush of blusher, a squirt of perfume. All this effort, and Jim Marston paid her not the slightest bit of attention. Next time I'll wear rockets in my hair, she promised herself grimly, and fire off a volley, one every ten steps!

But the sun was bright, as usual, and the sea spread before their feet in all its glory, and only the cloud-rimmed peak of Mt Soufrière, looming behind them, cast a shadow over the day.

The bus came on time, filled with chatter that almost drowned out the rattle of the chassis and the moaning of the engine. 'Hey, missy,' one of the female passengers yelled down to her. 'You still got that man? He any good at night work?' There was a roar of friendly laughter as two men helped bulky Bea up the ladder and into the compartment.

'You get tired of him, I gotta empty bed at my house,' another woman yelled. 'Mine!' And the bus drove off in a cloud of dirt and burned oil.

There was a teasing grin on Jim's face as the bus disappeared round the curve in the road. 'I didn't realise I was in such popular demand,' he drawled. 'They don't pull many punches.'

'That's all talk,' she told him firmly. 'Nothing but talk! But I must admit,' she added, 'that in the villages they tend to be a little more—frank about——'

'Sex?' he interjected. Peggy swallowed her tongue. Why in the world did *this* conversation have to appear? she asked herself. Maybe if I just ignore him it will go away. I hope. She crossed her fingers behind her back. 'The beach is just down that path,' she indicated, and

went striding off in that direction. The icicles on her
words would have made a penguin feel at home.

'I gather we're not going to talk about that other
subject?' Jim asked mournfully.

Pseudo-mournfully, Peggy told herself. He's having
the time of his life getting at me!

He offered her a little bow and followed her down the
path, making an occasional remark about the weather,
the bushes, and the varicoloured birds. None of his
statements required an answer. And I'm glad, she told
herself. This man is just too confusing. I don't know
whether to laugh or cry. But I suppose every man in his
line of work has that surface appeal? It seemed to be
the right answer, but she liked it not one little bit. When
they came out of the brush on to the fine-grained black
sand of the beach she stripped off her clothes and ran
for the waves, leaving the man to his own devices.

There was something about tropical waters—if the
presence of sharks, barracuda and other uncomfortable
neighbours were ignored. It seldom went below seventy
degrees Fahrenheit in the summer season, but since the
air temperature hovered around eight-five, the ocean was
coolly refreshing. Only a few yards away from them the
Wallilabou River came dashing down off the mountain.
Its cold, fresh waters carved a noticeable path out into
the heavier salt water, and then dissipated just beyond
the reefs.

Peggy, who had lived beside the ocean most of her
life, was as at home in the depths as any of its finned
residents. So she ran ahead until the water was almost
waist-deep, poised herself for an incoming breaker, dived
under it, and coasted out to sea like a sleek little porpoise.

She surfaced finally, a good distance out, shook her
head to relieve her ears, then turned over on her back
and then let the soothing ocean wash away all her

troubles. Occasionally she heard a shout in the distance, but ignored it by diving for the bottom, looking for conches.

But a guilty conscience was not something one can wash away permanently. So, about ten minutes after her initial plunge, she selected a good wave, rode it in, and abandoned it just as it was about to tumble her up on the beach. And Jim was standing there, a smile on his face.

'You should get a surfboard,' he told her.

She looked around quickly. A couple of the village children, too young to work, were busy building a sand-castle just above the tide-line.

'That's another one of those things aboard my treasure ship,' she assured him as she accepted the towel he handed her. 'Thank you, but you didn't have to watch the basket. These boys won't steal a thing.'

'They swim like little tadpoles,' Jim commented. 'If it weren't for the breakers they'd be Olympic class.'

'Yes,' she returned, thankful that he was not raining down a storm on her head. 'They all begin when they're about six months old. Up at the swimming pool.'

'Swimming pool?' he questioned.

'Up the mountain.' She busied herself drying her hair. He took the towel from her and began to rub gently. Another flash of feeling rumbled up along her spine. No one but her mother had ever dried her hair for her—and certainly her mother's touch hadn't had *this* effect on her. To maintain her poise, she talked faster.

'Not really a swimming pool,' she gabbled. 'Just a dammed-up little swimming hole. It's a fine place to swim. Hardly anyone can see; practically all the kids go skinny-dipping up there, only the stream comes right off the mountain, and it's colder than a witch's—er—it's frigid!'

'How frigid can it get'—he laughed—'in the middle of the tropics?'

'Well, I don't know,' she said. 'Papa measured the water temperature once at sixty degrees. But it was ninety degrees in the shade at that moment so, if you jumped in, there was a thirty-degree difference.' She snatched the towel back from him as his hands wandered out of her hair and down to her shoulders.

'Hot and cold are relative things, Mr Marston,' she said, very distinctly.

'Yes, I've noticed,' he chuckled. 'And since I'm hot I guess I'd better dive in and see about cooling down.'

'The very thing,' she advised him firmly. 'The very darned thing.'

He turned and rushed out into the surf, making a very credible racing dive. She watched eagerly for his head to appear. It took more time than it should, and her fingernails were biting into her palm when finally he surfaced. She relaxed with a huge sigh, and walked over to where the boys were adding a crooked turret to their castle.

'Darn man,' she muttered. The children looked up at her curiously. 'He's doing that just to tease me,' Peggy snapped. 'Or scare me. Maybe it's the same thing! Sometimes I'd like to go after him with a meat cleaver!'

One of the children was Joseph's son. Not more than four years old, he flashed her a brilliant smile. 'Is a fine man you got there, Miz Peggy,' he said. She looked down at him, thunderstruck by the judgement. The boys went back to their architecture as if they hadn't noticed that Peggy Mitchell's world had just been turned inside out!

# CHAPTER SIX

JIM MARSTON came out of the water just before noon, looking wet and sleek and incredibly agile. Peggy, stretched out on her beach towel, watched, intrigued by the maleness of him, the sheer sense of power and excitement he spread around him. The boys had long since given up their castle, and had gone wandering off looking for lunch.

'Nice work,' Jim announced as he circled the construction work. 'I've always wanted to wreck a castle.' With that, he jumped into the courtyard of the edifice and trampled the outer curtain walls with his bare feet.

A gull, walking the sand a few feet away, hurtled into the air, squawking. 'Now see what you've done,' Peggy chuckled. 'He wants the castle wrecked in his own way. A typical male, isn't he?'

'All my fault,' Marston returned as he abandoned his attack. 'You don't suppose he holds the local real estate franchise? Maybe I should kiss his foot—or yours?'

'Don't you dare!' she squeaked, as she rolled off her towel into the black sand and prepared to come up fighting—or running. 'I have no intention of being a stand-in for you and your birds. Settle your arguments among yourselves!'

He folded his arms across his chest and stared at her. 'You know, I have the suspicion that you're ticklish, Peggy Mitchell.'

'Don't you dare!' She began to back away from him warily. He began to stalk her, wearing a wide grin. Anger is a hard humour to maintain in the face of such a predator, Peggy told herself. The corner of her mouth curled up. Thinking she might outflank him with her native speed, she vaulted to her feet and made a dash to get by. But she hadn't counted on the speed of the man behind her. Hardly a foot beyond him a hand caught at her ankle and tumbled her. She ended up ploughing a furrow in the black sand.

'Gotcha!' Jim crowed as, having barely trapped her with his wild tackle, he scrambled forwards and pinned her with his weight.

'That's not fair,' Peggy complained. 'I can't wrestle my way out—my bathing suit is very fragile, you—you masher!'

'The only place I've ever heard that word is in 1930s movies,' he laughed. 'And this is where we tickle.'

He raised his index finger as if it were a sword, made a couple of artistic passes in the air, and then lightly touched her side, just below her lower rib. It must have been luck, Peggy thought. How else could he know that I'm ticklish only in that one spot? She stiffened her resolve, and her muscles, in a vain attempt to make no response.

'Not the right place?' he enquired pleasantly.

If she had tried to answer she would have laughed, and given the whole show away. So she pressed her lips tightly together and said not a word. His finger moved to the other side. 'Here?'

'No, darn you!' This part was easier; she never had a tickle-response on that side. His eyes lit up. He waved his finger in the air once more, and stabbed gently at the first spot.

There was no controlling her response. She gasped and laughed and roared and wriggled, all to no avail, until finally tears of laughter filled her eyes, and Jim Marston was close. So very close.

A stillness descended on them both at that moment. Some change had occurred. Jim was no longer tickling her, and a strange and powerful emotion had sprung up between the two of them. She brushed aside the tears and gasped for breath as his head came closer to hers, blotting out every other sensation.

'Peggy.' Not a question, not a statement, just the ragged soft sounding of her name, followed by his deep sigh, almost as if the air were being pumped out of his lungs. Her eyes widened. This was something she had not expected, had never experienced. Her hand came up in wonder and stroked his cheek gently, transferring more tactile flashes of—what? Peggy didn't know the word to apply, but she felt the emotion running up and down her spine. An awareness, where none had been before. His weight was on her, from toe to breast, but she hardly noticed. His hand riffled through her hair and down to her earlobe before it cupped her chin. 'Peggy,' he whispered again.

She could find no words to answer. Her throat was blocked by some emotional peak. She shivered down the whole length of her body as his hand moved to her breast, and then returned to the tie behind her neck that kept the old one-piece suit fastened in place. No. I should say no, she told herself dreamily. But—I don't want to. How about all those years, Miss Prude? Boasting about your virtue? But nobody had ever really challenged that vaunted virtue, had they, fool? Until now. How easy it's been, saying that you were just not interested! And now—you are interested, aren't you! Fool! What do you want now, missy?

I don't want him to stop, she confessed to herself, as she made no objection, and was carried away into the primal world of basic emotions.

There could be no measure of the time involved, or the place. All that had gone by the board, until gulls returned, dive-bombed the pair who were occupying their festival area, and squawked in their ears. The warning was just in time. A confusion of voices were racing at them, coming down the path from the village.

With a start Peggy snapped back to attention as Jim's hand halted, hesitated, moved, and then halted again. 'Oh, boy!' he muttered as he quickly re-tied the knot behind her neck and rolled off her. Down the path that led from the village to the beach a horde of little boys were running, yelling at the tops of their lungs. Only then aware of how heavy he had been, how bruising, Peggy struggled awkwardly to sit up, to regain her firm control over her own world.

'We—mustn't play that game again,' she managed to get out as she nervously tugged her suit into place.

'Do you want me to apologise?' he asked. There was something about his voice that was changed. Harder, Peggy thought. He's shut everything off, all his emotions, all his interest.

'No,' she sighed, trying to dismiss it all from her mind. 'No, it takes two to tango. But——'

'But you don't care to dance any more?'

'No,' she returned reflectively. 'And besides, we have to move off the playing field. Perhaps we could sit up there on that ledge and watch the boys while we have our lunch?'

He handed her up gently. 'That's probably the way to go.' He smiled grimly. 'When in doubt, eat lunch. Come on.' He snatched up the lunch basket and strode off up the incline to the grass just above the beach, leaving Peggy alone, first with her confused mind, and then with the mess she was making, trying to slide her clothes over her wet bathing suit.

'You know, putting your clothes on over a wet bathing suit won't solve any problems.'

'That's what you think,' Peggy muttered, 'but it's a step in the right direction. Now, if you would clear a space over there, we can eat. I suppose you wouldn't mind cold fried chicken?'

'Love it,' he laughed. 'Home cooking?'

'Yes,' she admitted. 'Colonel Sanders hasn't reached this end of the island yet.' She bustled as she unpacked the basket, glad to have something for her hands to do. It distinctly helped to control her nervousness.

'So we'll sit here and enjoy, and watch the baseball game?'

She looked up at him and laughed.

'You're not only in the wrong league, man, but the wrong culture. Cricket is the name of the game around this island.'

'Cricket? I don't know beans about cricket,' he groaned. 'But this chicken leg is good.'

'Not to worry,' she commented. 'Just lean back, Mr Marston, and I'll explain it all to you.'

'Hey, that's great! I've heard it said that cricket can be a boring spectator sport.'

'Never happen,' she told him. 'Now, just let me stretch out there in the shade and get comfortable, and I'll demonstrate.'

Marston leaned back against a scrub bush and relaxed. He had always had an interest in sport, but in this game the batsman never seemed to be out. And when he turned to his left to consult his resident expert, he found Peggy Mitchell fast asleep. It had been a long night for him, too. He smiled, and closed his eyes for just a moment.

*    *    *

A heavy hand rocked her shoulder gently. Peggy muttered a protest, and turned on her side, trying to punch her pillow into a more comfortable shape. The pillow immediately protested, and the hand shook her again. 'All right,' she grumbled, and opened one eye.

Her pillow was Jim Marston's shoulder, and the hand shaking her belonged to Henry, the blacksmith. The cricket team had disappeared, and the sun had marched across considerably more of the horizon than she remembered. She sat up, shoving Jim's hand away to do so.

'What——?' she stammered. 'I'm sorry, Mr—er— Jim. I didn't mean to fall asleep on you.'

'*I'm* not,' he chuckled. 'I loved every minute of it. Well, all those minutes that I can remember.'

'Missy,' Henry interrupted. 'They here. That bunch you tell me to watch for, they here.'

'Oh, lord.' Peggy scrambled to her feet, a feeling of panic running up her spine.

'No need to be excited,' Jim commented as he unfolded gracefully. 'Just *where* are they?'

'At the village,' Henry told them. 'You gotta get busy, man!' He pronounced it in the island fashion, *mahn.*

'I'm sorry,' Peggy interjected. 'Jim, this is Henry Coeurdeleon. Henry is the head man in these parts, and the foreman on my plantation.'

'I met Henry,' Jim responded, 'when I took my car into the village.'

'And I right pleased about them almond trees,' the big black man chimed in. 'Make a good living, that. Providing us got a market?'

'We'll have a market,' Jim assured him. 'Coeurdeleon, huh. The lion-hearted?'

'Just so.' The big man grinned. In a country where dentistry was a lost art, surprisingly, Henry had all his teeth. 'My granfa, you know. Or was it *his* granfa? I dunno. All us come here on the ships to be slaves, you know. And then when freedom come, why, we take the names as please us. You like that?'

'I like that very much,' Marston replied. 'In fact, you make me a little jealous. Now look, Henry, we have to sneak up to the house. Can you make some diversion—keep that bunch out of the way while we slip by? They must on no account see me!'

'Diversion?' The big man nibbled on his lower lip. 'You mean, like lead them around Sam Grover's barn?'

'Who the devil is Sam Grover?'

'He's nobody,' Peggy explained. 'That's a cliché. It means to—to lead someone down a false trail.'

'Just what I said,' agreed Jim. 'Lead them around Sam Grover's barn a couple of times, Henry.' The amiable giant grinned back at him.

Peggy stared at the two of them. Two arrogant, dominating males, she told herself with a giggle. Behold, we are the rulers of the world! Darned peacocks! They wouldn't know how to turn the daylight on without a woman to show them! Which was another local cliché, much loved in a free-speaking society.

'Give me ten minutes' head start,' Henry ordered, as he turned back up the trail. With a wave of his hand he disappeared into the brush, as quietly as a stalking lion.

'Well, now, we've ten minutes to spare,' Jim said. 'Now just do you suppose we could——?'

'Oh, no, we couldn't,' Peggy squealed, as she ducked and stepped away from him.

'Now look at that,' he told the world mournfully. 'She's running out on us. She doesn't want to play in the sand. Peggy's mad at me.'

'No, Peggy is not mad,' she assured him firmly. 'But Peggy isn't playing any more games with you. Not at all!' She stood up, brushed her drying clothes down, and started up the trail. Jim Marston watched for a moment, intrigued by her natural motion. Then he picked up the basket and followed. As soon as he started moving she turned to look at him over her shoulder. 'Watch your step here. This rock is slipping.'

He tendered a sarcastic little 'Ah,' and passed her up the trail, swinging the heavy basket on two fingers. Disgusting, Peggy thought, as she watched him zig and zag ahead of her. He moves around like a mountain goat, and me, the calves of my legs are already beginning to strain. You would think *he* was the one who walked this track every day for the past three years. Maybe I could fake a twisted ankle and he would carry me? The thought brought on giggles which were hard to suppress, and so she arrived at the house not only with tired legs, but almost completely out of breath, and plunked herself down on one of the wicker chairs on the porch.

Jim looked down at her as she caught her breath. A fine, feisty little girl, he thought. Not half bad-looking, by any means. But more than that—a completely natural woman who laughed when she was happy, cried when she hurt, and never seemed to deceive. The sort of woman a man could be happy with, right? The sort of woman any sensible man could fall in love with? The question startled him, as did the answer. True. All true.

He shook his head in disgust, not understanding his own emotions. His motto for years had been love them and leave them, but *that* wasn't the sort of love he was thinking of now. This kind of love had to do with *forever after*. 'And I'm not sure I'm ready for that,' he whispered to himself.

'I—don't think I'm ready for all this,' Peggy said. 'Are you going to stay with me?'

'No, that isn't the way this game is played,' he responded. 'All I do is set the stage for the two sides to bargain. You know what you have to sell, you know the price you want.'

'But I can't imagine why they would want to buy arrowroot,' she muttered. 'Everybody knows there's no world market for the stuff. I'd be cheating them——'

'Don't ever say that!' he replied roughly. 'It's purely a business deal. They know why they want it. You don't have to know. There's no dishonesty involved, Peggy.'

'You're sure?'

'Of course I'm sure. And think of what you have to gain. You want to preserve the plantation for your brother. You want to make a profit for the village and the co-operative. Here's the ideal opportunity, and all you have to do is keep your cool! Let's go inside and get settled.'

'Hello, the house!' They had left the porch just in time. Henry was outside, accompanied by a mismatched trio whom he ushered up the stairs. Peggy took a deep breath, smoothed down the red culottes, and walked to the door.

'Missy, this be Miss Vera Helst, Mr Wilson the lawyer, and Mr Johnson of Harriman & Son.' Henry did the honours as the three of them filtered past her guard. 'They come from Kingstown jus' to talk business.'

'Is that so?' She tried to make the welcome just a little bit chilly. The tall thin woman, inches taller than she, swept past Peggy disdainfully, her jet-black hair bobbing as she moved. Despite the long walk up the hill and 'around the barn', she still had that sleek, sophisticated look. No cracks showed in her painted face. Her predatory eyes roamed the house, scanning Peggy only briefly. For a moment Peggy felt embarrassed, standing there in her sandals and T-shirt, with a pair of wrinkled culottes over her swimsuit. She gestured the trio to chairs and stood stiffly in front of them.

Wilson seemed uncomfortable. He shifted his weight a couple of times and avoided her eyes. And that, Peggy thought, takes care of all my doubts. They deserve whatever they get! Henry, coming in behind them all, put a comforting hand on her shoulder. She looked up at him and offered a warm smile before she turned back to the visitors.

'So. You've come all the way from Kingstown on business? I can't imagine what we have that you might want.'

'That's what I like,' Vera said. She had manufactured a smile to go with the words, but of warmth there was nothing. It's like talking to a puppet-doll, Peggy thought. I wonder where the strings are?

'Yes,' the woman continued. 'I—ah—believe we can do you a favour, Miss Mitchell. A very big favour.'

'I certainly wouldn't fight that,' Peggy returned. 'Would you like some refreshment? Tea? I know it's a hot trip from town.'

'I'd rather get right to the point,' Vera commented.

'Then go ahead.' And make it quick and short, Peggy told herself. My courage is fast running out. Maybe I ought to run out into the kitchen and get my tank refilled?

'I represent an organisation in New York,' Mr Johnson interrupted. He was a big man, white-haired, red-faced, with a hawk beak and hunched shoulders that gave him the appearance of a vulture. Vera Helst withdrew from the conversation immediately. 'We are a—trading firm, Harriman & Son. You might perhaps know one of our competitors?'

'I'm afraid not, and I'm not sure what that all means,' Peggy muttered truthfully. 'I'm afraid I don't know a great deal about business.'

Henry squeezed her shoulder gently, Vera smiled a sort of barracuda smile, and Mr Wilson did his best to disappear into the chair cushions.

'You haven't met Mr Marston?' Vera asked.

'Oh. Him. Yes, I've met him,' Peggy admitted. 'He's in the trading business, too?'

'It isn't important,' Johnson said. 'Mind if I smoke?' At Peggy's shake of the head he brought out a massive cigar and lit up. 'Yes, well, we buy and sell,' he continued. 'We find suitable products, and match them to responsive markets. In your case, arrowroot.'

'My goodness, do you mean you want to buy our arrowroot crop? That's the second offer I've had in five days,' Peggy mused.

'An' we ain't even got half of it out of the ground,' Henry interjected. Now he's the one who should be doing the acting, Peggy told herself. Look at that big grin. Henry is every bit an island trader!

'Another offer?' Johnson suddenly abandoned his cultured poise as his nose sniffed possible trouble.

'Yes,' Peggy admitted. 'And very substantial, too. An offer to buy for cash, as is.'

'As is?'

'In the ground,' Henry added. 'That man, he buy it all, and then say he gonna contract with me to harvest. I don' mind. You talkin' the same?'

'As is?' Johnson fumbled with the briefcase clutched in his lap. 'Yes, of course. We'll buy the whole crop, as is. And offer you ten per cent more than your last offer.'

Peggy almost swallowed her tongue. Ten per cent more would make this the highest sale price for arrowroot that the island had ever seen.

'You know,' she stammered, 'that we have two hundred acres ready to harvest? And another crop twice the size in the barns?'

'Of course,' Vera acknowledged. 'And the only crop of arrowroot on the island this year, isn't that so?'

'That's for sure,' Henry avowed. 'Nobody else have the smart to plant the root this year. Only Miss Peggy.'

'I—ah—really have to have some tea,' Peggy said nervously, and before anyone could comment she was out of the room and into the kitchen, where Jim Marston was playing solitaire at the kitchen table. 'You heard?' she gasped.

'I heard,' he answered. 'Don't be too eager.'

'But—that's a fortune,' she stuttered. 'I—you think?'

'I think you deserve it,' he said unashamedly. 'You *do* know what they're going to do, don't you? First they're going to try to find out what *my* market is, and, if that doesn't work, then they'll try to stick me with a quick resale—at a decent profit, of course.'

'But——'

'But what?'

'But I don't have the nerve,' she sighed.

Marston shook his head and stood up. 'I can see you need a shot of Dutch courage,' he said.

'I don't want anything to drink! Good lord, I—I don't know what you're talking about,' she answered quickly, backing away, unfortunately into a corner.

'Yes, you do,' he laughed. 'You know exactly what I'm talking about, lady.' It seemed at the moment, to Peggy, that it was all true about the human brain being divided into two separate hemispheres. One of them was telling her to run; the other was telling her to pucker up. In receipt of both commands, her feet remained fixed in place, although occasionally her knees would jerk, first to one side, and then to the other.

'That little hula dance isn't necessary,' he gloated. 'The villain has you, missy.' As indeed he had. One of his big hands rested on either of her shoulders, pulling her gently forwards until the tips of her breasts grazed the front of his shirt. Then his right hand moved down across her back, tucking her gently into the curve of him.

She looked up, tears of excitement glistening in her eyes. His head came down slowly, until his two warm, moist lips touched hers. A gentle touch at first, and gone quickly as he withdrew, leaving her bereft. And then he returned to the work. Soft pressure, alarming contact, and all her fears fled. With a little squeak of enjoyment she squirmed closer and stretched upwards on the tips of her toes, so that her hands could encircle his neck and rest at his nape.

Soft, sweet pressure, not the sort that set the barn on fire, but rather that established a comforting closeness, followed by the gentle penetration by his tongue that told her he was the man she had been waiting for.

There was the sound of laughter from the sitting-room. It was enough to break them apart, she with a red face, he with an astonishing shortness of breath which he couldn't quite explain.

'Hey,' Marston objected. 'I'm not finished here.'

'Yes, you are,' she said firmly, pushing him off.

'But I've done a lot of work——'

'You only get what you earn,' she told him primly as she whirled around and headed for the door.

'Oops, you forgot the tea,' Jim Marston teased.

'The devil with the tea,' she whispered back at him. Her hand moved unerringly to that spot on the lower shelf of the cupboard where the bottle of Bacardi rum was kept. 'I think I'll provide some real lubrication.'

Vera was deep in conversation with Henry when Peggy came back into the living-room. They were hard at it, talking about labour contracts and schedules and high-speed harvesting. Wilson the lawyer was fumbling through a series of papers on his lap. Johnson sat back in his chair, looking like some benign Buddha.

'Don't mind if I do,' Johnson said, as Peggy set the bottle down on the side-table near him, and fetched some glasses from the sideboard. By the time the auxiliary bargaining was finished, the entrepreneur had already emptied his glass twice, and the lawyer was considerably ahead of him. Peggy nursed the tiny splash of liquid she had taken for herself. Although rum was the island drink, she had never acquired a taste for it, except as a very thin mixer.

'So,' Henry said. 'You pay by the hour, we finish in the week. Pay half up front, other half on day we finish. You provide trucks to move. OK?'

'OK,' Vera agreed, and then turned, smiling, to Peggy. 'I hope you don't feel put out. I realise that negotiating the harvest contract before you've signed the sale agreement is perhaps—a little hurried.'

'I'm still confused,' Peggy returned. 'You really want our arrowroot, as is, at that price?'

'Right here in the contract.' Johnson snatched the legal document from Wilson and held it out in Peggy's direction. 'I took the liberty of having the contract drawn up before we came, and we only have to add—right here—the price, as you see. And the labour contract is separate. Now if you'll just sign here—— '

A very loud crash from the kitchen disturbed everything. 'The dog,' Peggy gasped, and rushed for the door. Henry followed her and stood in the doorway, making sure that none of the other three could see into the kitchen.

'You broke a chair!' Peggy challenged as she looked at Marston.

'It's like the old mule story,' he whispered. 'First I had to get your attention. Look, don't sign a thing today. We have to go over that contract line by line. Tell them you have to think about it overnight. Tell them to come back tomorrow at this same time, with a certified cheque. Got that?'

'Certified cheque? What's that?' she gasped.

'Babes in the woods,' he muttered, moving closer. 'That's a cheque stamped by the bank, guaranteed of payment, even if the payer changes her mind. Once that cheque is in your hands it's as good as money. Certified cheque, got it!'

'I've got it,' Peggy murmured. 'Certified cheque. Certified cheque. Kiss me again.' He did.

'Wasn't nothin',' Henry announced as they rejoined the others. 'Lazy dog, that. Too lazy to walk around, they have to knock something over. Dogs and kids, heh?'

'You have a child, Miss Mitchell?' Vera enquired with all the subtlety of a dustcart.

'No, no child, but a dozen dogs,' Peggy said very firmly, with enough of a glare in her eye to close off that avenue of conversation.

'Yes, well.' Vera fumbled for a moment, recognising her own *faux pas*. 'And now, about signing this contract?'

'Signing?' Peggy did her best stupid-redhead impression as she bubbled along. 'Oh, I couldn't possibly sign anything without thinking it over. Sleep on it, that's what Papa always said. And besides, my lawyer...' She let the sentence die off and fade away.

'I'm sorry,' Johnson insisted, 'but time is of the essence. I couldn't possibly let the deal hang for more than twenty-four hours. I have to get back to the city, you know.'

'Why, that's just what I was thinking,' Peggy exclaimed in delight. 'Twenty-four hours. That will give me more than enough time to examine every little detail. Read all the fine print, isn't that what they say? So then, if you would return tomorrow at this time? I'm sure you would want to have an expert of your own examine the crop?'

'Good idea,' Johnson said. 'It's just what I had in mind. Tomorrow then?'

'Oh, yes, tomorrow afternoon,' Peggy chortled. 'And of course you'll bring a certified cheque for the total amount along with you?'

'Certified cheque?' Johnson took a deep breath. It wasn't at all what he had intended. The cheque, when it came, was to have been long after the resale, with lots of little hold-ups built in, so that Harriman & Son could complete the deal without really investing any of its own money.

'Oh, yes, certified please,' Peggy repeated. 'My father always insisted on it. Payment on the barrel-head, either cash or a certified cheque.'

With success so close at hand, Johnson was not about to renege. 'Of course,' he agreed. 'Until tomorrow, then. Mr Wilson?'

The lawyer barely managed to get to his feet, with the help of Henry's hand under his elbow. The rum bottle was half empty, the man was half full. 'Yesh,' he muttered. 'Nicetameetyall.'

'You'll feel better when we have walked down the hill to your car,' Henry assured him. 'I gonna take them back now, missy. You be sure to take care of everything up here.'

'There must be a short cut,' Vera Helst pleaded. 'That trip up here was interminably long.'

'Going downhill always easier,' Henry promised as he led them out of the house and down the trail. Peggy stood in the centre of the living-room, hands on hips, until they were out of sight. Then she whirled around and ran for the kitchen.

'They've gone,' she yelled. Jim Marston raised a cheer. Then he seized Peggy's tiny form, swung her round a couple of times, and hugged her close.

'You did wonderfully,' he murmured in her ear. The warmth of his breath, the strength of his arms, and the security she felt in his arms, all conspired against her. Without thinking, she kissed him.

He was not the first man who had ever kissed Peggy Mitchell, but as far as she could remember he *was* the first man she had ever kissed on her own initiative. As before, it was warm and moist—and promising. What, she wasn't quite sure, but it promised *something*! Peggy could feel the little shock that ran through her, as she hung there some inches above the floor. The security she felt in his arms! Just a phrase that had flashed through her mind a moment earlier, but containing all her problems and all their solutions. Since her father had so mysteriously disappeared, Peggy Mitchell, while showing an outward face of confidence, had secretly been seeking—security. And here it was, so strong, so over-whelming, that she sighed fretfully when he let her slide down to her own feet.

Quite suddenly her world seemed complete.

'There's only one problem,' she told him when, some hours later, they sat companionably on the porch watching the tropical stars. 'All this activity. All for a three-year crop of arrowroot? I just don't understand. You—and Harriman & Son too, I think—you're accustomed to dealing with bigger things than this. Much bigger.'

He reached over and patted her hand. 'You're right.' His deep, resonant voice sent little shivers up her back. 'But every good thing has to have some small beginning somewhere. This is a perfectly valid deal. A chance, based on the evidence they think they have, for them to get in on the ground floor.' He pulled her up to her feet and over to the screen mesh that kept the porch safe from insects.

With one arm around her, he nestled her head to his shoulder. 'If they are able to find the market, you'll see this bunch roaming the whole island, buying up options for future crops.'

'But if there won't be any market, and it'll all turn out to be a hum?'

'Well, that's the chance you take in the trading business,' he said. 'Who knows? Maybe they know something we don't know.' He squeezed her shoulder and explained about the possible use of arrowroot in the computer-paper business. 'And if that proves out,' he added, with a little chuckle, 'we will have done ourselves in, and they'll make a great profit. And that's what being an entrepreneur is all about. Guess right, and you make huge profits where none existed before. Guess wrong, and you lose a bundle.'

He gently pushed her round in front of him, both hands drooping lazily over her shoulders. 'But that's a story for another day,' he murmured into her hair. 'Tonight we have a tropical moon, brilliant stars, the perfumes of the world riding the wind, a beautiful woman——'

'And a beautiful man,' she interrupted. But for some reason—the sloughing of the wind in the banyan tree just outside, perhaps, or the sound of peeping from the tree frogs—the dream spell had been broken. Moving very slowly, almost regretfully, she pushed his hands aside and went back into the house. She hardly noticed the wry grin as he shoved both his hands in his pockets and began to whistle.

# CHAPTER SEVEN

MUCH to Peggy Mitchell's surprise, the technical expert appeared at sunrise on the following day, deep in conversation with Henry and a couple of the other men from the village. They all seemed equally surprised to find her on the steps of the porch, nursing her tea in the battered old mug that had served her for years. She was dressed in utilitarian black trousers and flowery blouse. Nothing ostentatious, but, then again, nothing to be embarrassed about. Her gleaming red curls bounced slightly as she moved, glistening in the early sun.

'Aye, missy,' Henry called. 'We don't expect to see you so early in the daylight.'

'What better time?' she chuckled, shifting into the soft English of the land. 'Chores all done, kitchen all clean, mos' best time sit and watch sunrise, no?'

Henry nodded his head. 'This here Mr Calderon, missy. Come on contract to look at the harvest, huh?'

'Mr Calderon.' She offered him a gracious acknowledgement and stood, leaving her mug on the step.

'My pleasure, ma'am.' Calderon was a tall thin man, a mulatto, with a shaven head and a slight stoop. 'I work at the factory in Belle Vue before they close. I don't know why the lady wants inspection. Everybody knows Mitchell plantation grows nothin' but the best. But they pay, so I go look. OK?'

Peggy knew without asking. The 'factory' was the old building where, when arrowroot was the crop of the entire island, the washed tubers fresh out of the ground were shaved and then pulped for shipment. But the failed arrowroot market had closed the plant, and thrown a dozen highly skilled employees out of work.

'Look everywhere,' she told him sincerely. 'Touch, see, feel. Make yourself welcome at Mitchell plantation—and then come and share tea, Mr Calderon.'

'Lady Bountiful?' Jim Marston had come out of the house behind her, as the men walked away. He was dressed in shorts and tropical shirt, water still gleaming in his hair. Peggy caught her breath at first sight. He was not handsome; what man really looked that well early in the morning? But there was so much virility about him, so much chained-down poise and strength, that she could not help but notice. His direct stare embarrassed her, and she turned away to keep him from reading her mind through her eyes.

'Bountiful?' she laughed. 'Not hardly. Land poor is what I am, if you like to have a description.'

'I'd rather have breakfast,' he coaxed.

'Men!' Her mother had always said that, in just such a disgusted tone, which merely served as a cover for love. 'And I suppose I'm to be the kitchen slave who runs instantly to get it?'

'Couldn't have said it better,' he chuckled. She blushed again and tried to sidle by him, but his quick hand clamped over her wrist. 'But a well-trained kitchen slave would at least have offered to kiss the master.'

'I did that last night and got in all manner of trouble,' she maintained stoutly. 'There's a union rule in this house. No kissing before sunset.'

'Cruel,' he muttered, but he loosened his grip and instead settled for a quick pat on her flank as she hustled by.

'Hey,' she complained, but kept going.

The first thing you know, he told himself, is that they're going to certify me as civilised and put a Grade

A stamp on my bottom. Can you imagine what the people in New York would say if they could see me now? Wolf Marston, doing good deeds, riding to the rescue? When did I ever go to these lengths before? Not only is it ridiculous in a man who hasn't had a decent thought in years, but damned if I'm not enjoying it! And again that vagrant thought struck him. What the devil is *love* all about? Not anything that *I'm* familiar with. Good lord, wouldn't my sister love to know that?

Peggy looked up from the frying-pan as he walked proudly in, and felt just that. Proud. My man. If only he could fall in love with me, she told herself wistfully. Wouldn't *that* be a wonderful ending? I should have asked Bea to read the cards for me! But deep in her mind was a shadow. I'm a terrible judge of men, aren't I? Starting with Papa. Bea was probably right about Papa, and she's probably right about Jim Marston— only I don't know *what* she thinks about Jim!

'Daydreaming women usually burn breakfast.' He was at her ear without her noticing his crossing the kitchen floor.

'Is that all you think about women?' she asked in a brittle voice. 'How useful they are in the kitchen?'

He moved even closer. She felt his warm breath on her neck. 'Not me, missy,' he whispered. 'I'm smarter than the average bear. I could hire a cook *any* day. Now where I want you——'

'I don't want to hear that!' she snapped nervously, moving away from him in agitation. 'Sit down at the table—please?' There was a strained, pleading look on her face. He shook his head mournfully, shrugged his shoulders, and moved away.

'Sooner or later,' he murmured.

'Not in *this* lifetime,' she promised him, as she dished out the scrambled eggs. He laughed, as if he were privy to some cosmic joke.

Mr Calderon and his cohorts were back at the house by noontime. Which was, of course, typical of workers in the tropics. High noon always represented a pause in the day. A pause for lunch, followed by a siesta. The tag that 'mad dogs and Englishmen go out in the noonday sun' had absolutely no application in St Vincent. Both the mad dogs and the Englishmen were already looking for a place to lie down before the sun hit its zenith. Peggy, alerted by dog barks, met them on the porch and offered cold drinks.

'Everything's of the best in the fields,' Calderon reported. 'Never have I seen better arrowroot. And all easily harvested, Miss Mitchell. You did a good job in the planting.'

'Well, I had a great deal of help,' Peggy stammered. 'And my father—he planned it all out, just before he—some time ago. But you plan to report to Miss Helst that everything is all right?'

'Just so,' Calderon said. 'I have a car in the village. I go back to K-town to make my report. Then I understand Miss Helst comes out this afternoon and completes the purchase. What I don't understand is, what they gonna do with all this arrowroot? Best I know, you couldn't sell ten pounds any place in the world. Be nice if the trade lives again. Those were the good times.' He shook his head and grinned at her before adding, 'Plenty people watching this deal. Everybody knows, all over the island. Fastest spread of gossip I ever see, this. *Somebody buyin' arrowroot!* I hear that all the way from K-town to Fancy.'

Peggy looked across at Jim, a stricken look on her face. 'I—hadn't counted on—raising everyone's expectations,' she sighed. 'I don't know that there's any market. I don't, honestly.'

'You don't gotta know.' Calderon laughed. 'This Miss Helst, she works for the big boys in New York. *They* the ones to worry about the market, not you nor me, lady. Not to worry. She bring cheque today. You trade it at the bank like pure gold. One week to harvest, two days to move. I hear they rent space in the old Wilson sugar warehouse to store. So everything OK. Everything out of our hands. You put in more arrowroot?'

'Well, maybe we think it over,' Henry commented. 'I say to missy, we work the land too hard for three years. Maybe let it lie fallow a time.'

'For this sale price,' Calderon grinned, 'you could afford to. Invest it in the land, Miss Mitchell. Buy fertilisers. Let it lay. Good idea. Well, I gotta go. Need to get back to K-town by one o'clock, you understand.'

'I understand.' Peggy forced a smile to her lips and saw the party off.

'I watch, bring that woman up so soon she shows up,' Henry said softly as he walked by her. 'But not too soon, huh? I send a boy ahead of us.' Peggy kept that artificial smile on her face until the party disappeared down the trail, but it was a suddenly sober woman who came back into the house.

'Second thoughts?' Jim asked.

'Third thoughts,' she sighed. 'It seems—now—Jim, are you sure that this is an honest business deal? I couldn't go through with it if I thought there was some—trickery involved. I think—I just can't go through with it so cold-bloodedly. When they come back, I'm going to warn that Miss Helst.'

'Go ahead.' He shrugged his shoulders as if it meant nothing at all. 'She won't give up the deal, you know. Oh, she might try to badger you into settling for a lower price, but she won't cancel out. They never do.'

'You don't care?'

'Me? Why should I care? Of course, I'll miss our nominal fee, but that won't break my back. No, Peggy, you're the one who'll suffer from it.'

'I don't understand.'

He got up and stretched, looking as if he were about to leave. She half stretched a hand in his direction, and stopped. 'No, it's your dream, Peggy. Your chance to give the Co-operative a big boost, your chance to diversify the plantation for the future, your chance to spruce things up and bring your brother home to his inheritance. All yours.'

'Oh, God,' she muttered, gnawing on her knuckles. 'But if it isn't honest?'

'Don't kid yourself,' he assured her. 'It's honest. There's risk in every business deal. This one is as honest as the day is long. Are you planning to upset the apple-cart, and let everything run into the sewers?'

'We don't have sewers—except in Kingstown,' she muttered.

'So? Are you going to tell Helst that it's a crook deal?'

Peggy took a step or two back and forth, and then dropped into Bea's rocking-chair. The rocker squeaked as she propelled it back and forth, and she almost doubled over with the concentration. Until at last, her mind made up, she halted the chair's movement and stared up at him. He was standing in front of her, his feet spread and his hand on his hips. And the look on his face was as honest as the day is long.

'No,' she said. 'I'm not going to say a word. *Caveat emptor*. Isn't that what the Romans used to say?'

'Let the buyer beware? That's still one of the basic laws of business,' he laughed. And that, Jim Marston thought, is one classy lady. He watched her walk down the hall, her hips swaying in a delightful tease, and licked his lips as if he could already taste it all.

As the afternoon passed, silence descended on the sleeping house. Except for Jim Marston, who still operated at New York time and speed. And what *he* was thinking as he rocked back and forth in the porch hammock would have surprised all his business associates back in the Big Apple. Or perhaps it wouldn't.

Peggy managed to wake up just before five o'clock. The heat of the summer day had invaded the house, leaving her soaked with perspiration. She gathered up a dress and undies and dashed for the shower. The normally cold water had been sun-warmed as it sat in the feeder tank on the roof. It cooled and cleaned and cheered her immensely. A few minutes later, wearing a simple blue cotton dress, she sauntered out to the porch, where Jim was immersed in a multi-page document. 'No nap?' she asked.

'Couldn't afford one,' he laughed. 'You've no idea how many people can sneak up on you when you're napping. I manage to survive on five or six hours of sleep a day—never more.'

'Good lord,' she muttered. 'No wonder I'm not in your line of work! That looks like serious reading?'

'It's your contract with little Miss Helst,' he said. 'The little lady has tried to slip two or three things over on you. I crossed out the applicable paragraphs in indelible ink.'

'And what does that lead to?'

'You just sign on the bottom, on the last page, and put your initials on every place that I've inked out. When the lady shows up, you just point them out. If she agrees, she initials the cross-overs too. If she doesn't agree, you just tell her there's no sale.'

'But then she might just walk out!' Peggy wailed.

'Oh?' He grinned up at her, leaning back as he did so. 'Aren't you the one who was so doubtful about all this? You had to be sure to warn her, and all that?'

'Yes,' Peggy snapped. 'But I changed my mind. And I'm not the type of woman who goes around in her mind like a revolving door. But——'

'But you'd like to make the sale?' He was wearing that sarcastic look again.

'Well . . .' she said hesitantly. 'Yes. Wouldn't anyone? All that money, and a chance to pay off the farmhands. And maybe send a little something to Andrew at college? He might be able to give up his job and concentrate on getting honours grades for his final year!'

'Didn't I tell you?' he chuckled. 'Greed triumphs over most anything.'

'Oh, you——' she snorted, and moved away from him. 'You'd never understand!'

'I understand all right.' He had moved up behind her quietly. 'And that's what the trouble is, isn't it? You hate for me to understand so clearly.'

'You think everything can be had for money, don't you?' she muttered bitterly.

'Yes.' She turned slowly round and looked searchingly at him. There was so much good in him, and yet he kept it all hidden beneath that cynical front of his. And, oh, how I wish I could break down his barriers! she thought.

'Not everyone is like that,' she sighed. 'Not everything is pure black or pure white. There are a million shades of grey, a thousand and one reasons, all valid in a person's mind, but beyond *your* ken.'

'I'm sure there are,' he agreed amiably, but she could see from the look in his eyes that he was only saying, not believing. 'I have to milk the goats,' she muttered, and ran back into the house to pick up buckets.

Twenty minutes later he joined her down by the barn. His 'good cheer' face was back on. 'Need any help?'

'Did you ever milk a goat?'

'*Milk* a goat? Missy, until I was fourteen I thought all milk came in plastic containers right from the tree.'

'So would you like to try?' He shrugged his shoulders, and took her place on the three-legged stool. She leaned over his shoulder to give directions. 'Gerda is a placid goat,' she warned, 'but you understand you're just coaxing her to give milk, not trying to pull her udder off!'

'So I'm the new kid on the block,' he laughed.

Yes, she told herself, still leaning over his back. That's one of the troubles. And why don't I move away from you, instead of resting against your warmth? Stupid woman!

'And you're supposed to hit the pail,' she continued indignantly.

'All right, all right. I'm learning. Lord, I had forgotten what nags women can be. Is Gerda your only milking goat?'

'No,' she giggled. 'We also have Harriet, but she hasn't come fresh yet. This isn't too much work, is it?'

'It's a terrible strain,' he admitted, 'but I suppose I can stand up to it. What happens when Gerda's empty? Is there a red light that comes on, or something?'

'That's silly,' she told him, as she moved away. 'When the milk stops coming, that's the end. Go too far and Gerda will tell you about it.'

'Well, how about that?' He chuckled. 'I guess I've gone far enough. Great experience.'

'That's nice,' she teased. 'Only it has to be done twice a day, seven days a week. Care to sign on?'

'What are you telling me? That a farmer's work is never done?'

'Exactly. Now, if you——'

But whatever it was she intended to say went by the board. Out at the front of the house Henry Coeurdeleon's big bass voice yelled, 'Hello, the house!' Pepper, the old dog, began to bay and made a mad dash for the front porch.

'Oh, God, they're here,' she gasped.

'Now don't come apart at the seams,' Jim cautioned softly. 'There's nothing out of order. You're the farm-woman, doing the chores. Just take the milk bucket and go ahead. I'll sneak in the back of the house. The con-tract is on the swing. Don't forget. She has to initial the cross-overs!'

'I'm—scared,' Peggy moaned.

'Of course you are. Here now, buck up.' He aban-doned the stool and came over to her. All her suspicions and doubts disappeared as he enveloped her within the safe shelter of those brawny arms, and his head came down towards hers. A gentle kiss this time, a touch on her lips, and then movement as he nibbled at the lobe of her tiny ear. 'There's no need to be afraid,' he whis-pered. 'No need to be afraid.' When his warm breath disappeared she moaned an objection.

But he had not withdrawn, merely shifted his aim back to the soft roundness of her lips. A shaft of pure joy zoomed up her spine. She relaxed and let him do his thing. Moments later, gasping for breath, he turned her loose. 'There now,' he murmured.

'Yes,' she sighed. 'Oh, dear, yes. You won't leave me?'

'Not for a minute.' She ducked her head into the security of his chest and blushed. He let her rest there for a moment and then pushed her away. 'Go get 'em,

tiger,' he chuckled, and turned her around before he gave
her a little push.

'Yeah, go get 'em,' she acknowledged, not too bravely.
'But if anyone yells at me I'm going to run!'

'Only as far as the kitchen,' he assured her. 'Get with
it.' So she did.

It was hard to know what activity most terrified Vera
Helst, but there was no doubt the woman was affected
by simple things. Pepper was making menacing noises
at her shapely feet. Preposterous, because Pepper had
teeth troubles; he might gum a visitor to death, but never
bite.

And the man standing there so patiently at Vera's
elbow might just as well have carried a sign on his back—
danger! About six feet tall, his muscular frame was en-
cased in a three-piece grey suit, and he possessed a broad
intelligent face, with wavy white hair. He was the epit-
ome of a successful world-class businessman. Vera Helst
was making as much effort to keep out of the stranger's
living space as she was to avoid the dog. When she saw
Peggy coming around the corner of the house with her
milk-pail in hand, Vera's face lit up and she brushed aside
all her other fears.

'Miss Mitchell!' She exuded goodwill like a maple tree
oozing sugar-sap. 'I'm sorry we couldn't get here earlier.
This is Mr Bardon.' The white-haired man made an el-
egant half-bow. 'Mr Bardon is from our New York
office. He is a specialist in these types of operation, and
a partner in the firm.'

Peggy looked him over slowly. The man was too neat
to be true, and there was about him an aura that reminded her of—Jim Marston! My lord, she thought,
another predator! Older than Jim, of course. Heavier.
But the same sort of man. One who had his eye on profits
first, and humanity later. Much later. Another bar-

racuda! God help me, she prayed silently. What would Bea say? We are fallen among thieves? Peggy carefully crossed the fingers of her free hand behind her back. 'I'm glad to meet you, Mr Bardon,' she lied. 'Why don't you come up to the house?'

They trailed behind her as if she were the Pied Piper, Mr Bardon almost at her elbow, Vera Helst at a safe distance behind him, Pepper bringing up the rear. And Henry was waiting for her on the porch.

'Ah, Henry.' It was so nice to see a friendly face that she almost bubbled over.

'Thought you might be napping,' the huge black man said. 'So I went through to the kitchen. Everythin' in good shape there, missy. Somethin' tell me to stay for the discussion, that's what.'

Something, or somebody? Peggy asked herself. In either case, I thank you, God. Or Jim, whichever comes first! 'That's a good idea, Henry,' she acknowledged. 'Won't you all be seated? It's cooler out here on the porch. Could I offer you a drink of some kind?'

They seated themselves, and accepted a drink.

Twenty minutes later, above the sound of ice clinking in their glasses, Mr Bardon began his inquisition. 'You've decided to sign the contract, Miss Mitchell?' He had a deep organ voice, which he played seductively. Unfortunately, Peggy was too frightened to be a ready target.

'With some small objections, yes,' she said. Her voice wavered on every other word. She swallowed hard, trying to hide her difficulty. 'It's over there on the hammock.'

Vera Helst snatched at the document, and began leafing through the pages. 'I understand that you met my friend, Jim Marston,' Bardon continued gently, casually, as if he were not entirely interested in the answer.

'I—yes,' Peggy returned as her brain clicked into action. That's what he wants to know. Not about any sales contract, but about Jim! 'Yes,' she repeated, and let her imagination run. 'Mr Marston seemed to be very interested in our area. I'm not exactly sure why. He spent two or three days here on the farm. And then—well, when he found out that my mother had died and I was all alone on the plantation without any idea about marketing our crops—he, well, he offered a substantial price for our arrowroot.'

'Did he do that?' Bardon returned musingly. 'But, of course, Marston is noted for his many charities.'

And here is where I turn it on, Peggy told herself. 'Charities?' she asked. 'Do you really think so? I thought that I—knew him better than I did. He came out to the plantation directly after he landed in Kingstown. Almost as if he knew where it was, and who we were.'

'Did he really?' Bardon commented. 'Well, he is an aspiring trader. A bit young, and perhaps not too attuned to people's sensitivities. Because of his youth, you understand.'

'A little too young—a little too brash,' Peggy said angrily, hoping that her voice was loud enough to be heard in the kitchen. 'In the end he became very—vulgar. I had to—he was much too personal. I finally—asked him to leave, you know. I have a large crop to sell, but I certainly didn't mean to include any extras in the contract. Besides, I've had another offer.'

Bardon's face lit up. 'You mean another besides ours?'

'Oh, yes.' Peggy turned her head away. This lying was becoming too easy. She was getting to *enjoy* lying to these people. 'An old Chicago firm, Simon & Poke, has tendered an offer.'

'Simon & Poke?' Bardon was still being casual. He looked over at Vera, who had completed her examination of the contract.

'Lawyers,' Peggy explained.

'Ah. Acting for someone else.' Bardon chuckled. 'Someone who doesn't want his name to be known.' Peggy shrugged her shoulders, getting deeper and deeper into her plot.

'I suppose,' she returned. 'But they offered a great deal of money. More than your offer, but—I prefer to deal with people face to face, you know, and that's why—well, you know. Another drink?'

Bardon nodded gracefully. Vera Helst offered a fluttery agreement. Peggy started to get up, only to have Henry intervene. 'I make the drinks,' the big man said. Since he knew the house as well as he knew the plantation, Peggy could see no logical reason to object. But she wanted very badly to get off the porch. Her courage needed renewing. So when Pepper wandered in on unsteady legs, a rim of chocolate something around his mouth and on the tip of his long hound-nose she was glad for the relief.

'This is Pepper,' she offered as an introduction, 'who has become so old that he actually thinks he's a house dog—which he isn't. Shoo, Pepper. Outside.' She held the screen door open. The old dog went, but reluctantly. 'Oh, lord,' Peggy added. 'Was that chocolate on his muzzle? Do you suppose he's been into the cake I made this morning?'

She turned to her guests with hands widespread in apology. 'I'm afraid you'll have to excuse me,' she said. 'You never know what goes on in your kitchen behind your back. I'm afraid I've a catastrophe out there.' With one hand she picked up the milk-pail. Before her guests could answer, she darted into the living-room and headed for the kitchen door at full speed.

Henry, busy mixing drinks at the little corner bar, winked and beckoned. She swirled to a halt, splashing a little milk out of the pail.

'Give them time to stew,' the big man said softly. 'Listen at that. They're in an argument already.' He nodded his head in the direction of the kitchen. 'Git,' he chuckled. 'When we get finished this deal, my Ada want you and you man to come down to the village for supper? And stay overnight for celebration?'

'If there's anything to celebrate,' Peggy responded. 'And he's *not* my man!'

'I hears you say that,' the big black man mocked.

'Well, all right,' she agreed, and stepped around him and his tray of drinks. Jim Marston pounced on her as she came through the door, swirled her round, and totally ignored the little squeak of alarm that she mustered.

'Peggy, you are some sort of miracle worker,' he whispered at her as he swung her round again. Despite all her prior doubts she felt a little tinge of pride warm her face and neck. 'We couldn't have done better if we'd hired Jane Fonda to act for us!'

Peggy lost her little smile. It was a bad comparison. After all, Madonna and Cyndi Lauper were more *her* generation and style! 'Put me down,' she muttered. 'You're making me dizzy, and I was dizzy enough when I came in!'

'Well—prickly cactus' he laughed, but set her down none the less. 'You've got just the angle. Work it for all it's worth, missy.'

'I've worked it past what it's worth already,' she mourned. 'I'm scared. I don't know what to say next! I think that in another five minutes I'll need smelling salts!'

'What you need,' he said, grinning, 'is another one of my patented kisses. Pucker up.'

'I'd rather have a piece of cake,' she said, challenging him.

'After,' he said. 'After.' His arms trapped her, and then he got down to the real work. For a few minutes—what seemed to be ages—Peggy hung in his arms and learned courage from his lips. When it was over—so quickly over—she stood with both feet flat on the floor and took deep breaths to settle herself. 'Why, it's dark,' she exclaimed, getting her first glimpse out the windows. 'What do I tell them now?'

'You need to run out more line,' he instructed. 'Tell them that I've called and apologised, and that as far as you know I'm up in Georgetown now, visiting with the Governor-General.'

'But *he* never goes to Georgetown,' she gasped.

'Hey, I'm writing the script!' He laughed. 'For today, he's gone to Georgetown with me to inspect some land. Got that?'

'I've got it,' she murmured. 'I'm going to have to spend weeks and weeks after this on my knees in church. I don't remember *when* I've told such awful lies before. And, for goodness' sake, don't eat any more cake. I made that for a birthday party tomorrow!'

'I'll watch your cake,' he promised, and there seemed to be a chuckle behind his words, something boding no good for the cake. 'I'm glad to see that you're not perfect, missy. I don't know how much longer I could put up with sainthood.'

'What did you mean by that?' she snapped.

'Look, honey,' he muttered. 'The business of the Church is the forgiveness of sin. Where would we all be if everyone was as innocent as you *seem* to be? Somebody has to sin, so we can be forgiven!'

Peggy stared at him, mouth hanging half open, astonished. 'That's a very strange view of Christianity you have,' she sighed as she turned round, squared her shoulders, and marched back out to battle.

Her guests were still waiting, their glasses refilled for the second time. Mr Bardon stood up. Peggy, whose brothers would never do such a thing, was startled, but managed to regain her seat.

'Lovely area,' Bardon commented as he waved his glass out at the scenery. There were still a few touches of light, reflections of sun off the towering peak of Mt Soufrière, which loomed behind them.

'Yes,' Peggy agreed. 'It's all lovely here. A beautiful, fruitful island. Do you know St Vincent very well?'

'My first visit,' he acknowledged, 'but not my last. Is it like this everywhere?'

'Oh, no,' Peggy hastened to assure him. 'On the Atlantic side it's all rocky shores and surf. Over here on the Caribbean side it's different. Why, over at Georgetown——' She clapped a hand over her mouth, as if remembering.

'Something?' Bardon enquired casually.

'That—Marston. Jim Marston,' she stammered, getting back into her part. 'I remember now. He said he had to go to Georgetown, over on the Atlantic coast, near the Orange Hill estates. Something about how he and the Governor-General were going to inspect a land project. And then——' her mind fumbled for something more to say '—and then he had to sail down to Beckwee to meet some Japanese—that's all I remember.'

Bardon's face lit up, even in the semi-darkness of the porch. 'Some Japanese,' he gloated. 'Where is this—Beckwee? I don't remember seeing it on the sailing charts.'

'Beckwee.' Henry laughed. 'You don't see it on charts. Missy been too long on the island. The charts says

Bequia. Pronounced Beckwee. Not far. A couple hours' smooth sailing to Port Elizabeth.'

'Well, I can't say that we're much interested,' Bardon said. 'We have what we want right here, Miss Mitchell. Now, Miss Helst and I have gone over all the changes you want in the contract, and initialled them, and we see no reason to delay. If you would sign here?' He whipped out an ornate gold fountain pen and handed it to her.

'I—don't mind signing,' Peggy stammered, 'but there was something about the money?'

'The money, of course. Give her the cheque, Vera!' The cheque duly changed hands. Henry came over to her chair and lit the lamp. Peggy examined the cheque in leisurely fashion, trying to act as if she understood everything it said, even though her hands were shaking with excitement. All she actually was able to read was the dollar numbers, with a fantastic series of zeroes after them, and the bank's certification stamp.

'Yes,' she muttered. 'Everything seems to be all right. I'll just sign my name here, shall I?' Her hand shook so badly she could hardly form the letters. Bardon, looking more and more like somebody's kindly uncle, added his signature to hers.

'And now,' he said as he rose and bowed over her hand in courtly fashion, 'I think Vera and I need to get on about our affairs. It's been a pleasure doing business with you, Miss Mitchell.'

Vera Helst, hanging on every word, smiled for the first time since the pair of them had arrived. 'Yes,' she added. 'It's been a very profitable visit.'

'I get a torch to lead you down,' Henry said as he stood up, towering over them all. He ducked into the house, and came back out with a flare torch in one hand.

'How quaint,' Vera Helst said. 'Torches. I suppose the natives dance in the moonlight?'

'I wouldn't be surprised,' Peg answered through her fatigue, thinking, How far out can this woman be? But she waved to the pair of them anyway.

'I couldn't tell you about the dances, of course,' she called after them. 'It's all voodoo, and women aren't allowed to watch. Goodnight!'

She leaned against the jamb of the door and watched the torch light them on their way. 'Good lord! What have I done!' Her frown fought with her giggles, and the giggles won!

# CHAPTER EIGHT

'HAVE they gone?' Jim came out of the kitchen cautiously, a big grin on his face.

'Yes,' she whispered. And then, in a tremendous shout, *'Yes!'* The certified cheque became a banner of triumph as she waved it over her head and danced around him. *'Yes!'* she yelled over and over again until, completely out of breath, she fell into his arms and giggled.

'I've never seen so much money in one place in all my life,' Peggy gasped. 'Is it real? It *must* be real. How can it be real?' Puzzled, she leaned back in his arms, and a frown formed. 'I don't think it's honest,' she sighed.

'OK, give me the cheque,' he offered. 'It's still not too late for me to run and catch up with them. I'll give it back, shall I?'

'Don't you dare!' she yelled at him, and backed away, waving the cheque in front of her.

'I'm not going to take it,' he laughed. 'I know it must seem like a fortune to you. I just wanted to call to your attention what you've done, my dear. Greed triumphs, even with lovely mountain girls like Peggy Mitchell!'

She was instantly sober. 'Yes,' she admitted slowly. 'That's true, isn't it. Lying, cheating, stealing! All those homely virtues I've nourished for years—they're all tumbling like Humpty-Dumpty! But I'm not going to give it back! I'm not!' When she looked up at him he could see tears in her eyes. 'I'm not,' she muttered.

'Of course you're not,' he agreed solemnly. 'It's an honest bargain. They went into it with their eyes open. They're a lot more greedy than you, missy. For them, this purchase is just a beginning. They have big plans to skin the world. From where I stand, theirs is major-league greed; yours is only small-time. Now come on. While you've been out here wheeling and dealing, I've been in the kitchen making us a grand supper.'

'You can cook?' If he had said that he could walk a tightwire one hundred feet up she could not have been more astonished. It was enough to take her mind off the previous conversation.

'Of course I can cook,' he said. 'Oh, ye of little faith—isn't that out of the Bible?'

'Yes, I suppose,' she returned, 'but there aren't any recipes in the Bible, for all I know.'

'Hey, cooking is a basic vocational skill,' he boasted. 'If any woman can do it, any man can do it better. All it takes is a little practice.'

'You bet,' she said sarcastically. 'Show me.' When he tucked her tiny frame under his arm she went willingly, glued to his side. Their lockstep was interrupted at the kitchen door; it wasn't wide enough for the pair of them to enter side by side.

The table was already set, gleaming cutlery and sparkling plates reflecting the light of the two tall candles in the middle of the display. 'Why, that's magnificent,' Peggy said in awe. 'How did you——?'

'I had plenty of time,' Jim answered, with a wry look. 'I had to do something. It was pretty nerve-racking to stand around listening to you people trying to con each other. Sit over here, missy.' He helped her to a chair, and then smiled down at her. 'I'd love to have a butler to help, but lacking that, here goes.'

The meal was much, much more than she could have anticipated. Calaloo soup, the island favourite made from black beans and pork; curried shrimp with a side-dish of peas and rice; a native lobster salad, along with fried plantains, a tomato, onion and cabbage salad—all washed down with rum punch spiced with nutmeg. Peggy ate heartily. Jim had concocted the best of everything that St Vincent provided. Only the rum punch bothered her. She was thirsty, and yet not too fond of alcohol.

'Too good to be true,' she chided him when the last vestige was devoured. And then, slipping into the island patois, 'How you know to do dis, man?'

'Well, to tell the truth,' he admitted, laughing, 'I had a little assistance. Ada, Henry's wife, sneaked in the back door to listen to the conversation, so she couldn't help but volunteer to help with the meal. Have another drink, missy? One last toast to good times?'

'Why not?' The alcohol had relaxed but had not intoxicated her. The artificial high imposed on her by the negotiations had been followed by depression at the thought that she might have cheated. The rum punch soothed all that, mixed all her emotions and left her with a bland, untroubled conscience. She felt wonderfully free of concerns and worries, for the first time in many a month. The pall cast over her life by her mother's death, her father's flight, all this faded away, and for a time there was only the circle of candlelight, the coolness of the night wind, the strength of this man in front of her.

'Coffee?' he offered.

'Why don't we have it out on the porch?' she responded. 'After we do the dishes. You can't leave a dirty dish lying around, not in the tropics. The bugs would be all over them in a shot. Wash or dry?' The look he gave her seemed to indicate that neither choice appealed, but he set to work beside her without a complaining word. With four hands, the washing-up went quickly.

'Take your cup. I'll bring the pot,' he said when the dishes were stacked and put away. The little procession made its way through the living-room. Peggy paused for a moment. 'It will be fun, being able to fix all this up the way it should be.'

'As it should be,' he agreed. Peggy smiled over her shoulder at his dark shadow and they went out on to the screened porch.

The tropical night held a subtle mystery. The moon hung low in the sky, seeming almost close enough to touch, sometimes yellow, sometimes gleaming silver. The stars were equally close and clear, a sparkling background against which the goddess of the night drove her way from horizon to horizon. And the wind, blowing off the sea, came laden with scents. The ginger clarity of the hibiscus, the touch of flavour from the banana, the cinnamon tree, the guava, all mixed together in nature's cocktail, prepared to seduce the senses.

Jim Marston settled into the hammock. She could hardly see him in the darkness, but knew he was there. She chose the armchair, pulling her feet up underneath her as she inhaled the marvels of the night, watched the moon, made a wish on a falling star. What do you wish, Peggy Mitchell? I wish that this time could go on forever. I wish that there never be a change. I wish that he would love me as much as I love him! A soft sigh escaped and gave her away.

'What are you thinking of, Margarita?' Such formality, such passion in a male voice. She could not deny him an answer.

'A long chain of things,' she told him softly. 'A night like this in Puerto Rico, and a boy I thought I loved.'

'What was his name?'

'I don't remember. I was fourteen then, and I was in love.'

'Or at least you thought you were?'

'Or at least I thought I was.'

'So what happened that night so long ago?'

'Nothing,' she sighed. 'That's why I remember it so well. Nothing happened.'

'Ah.' She heard faint noises in the darkness, and suddenly he was beside her, sitting on the solid arm of the chair, his hand ruffling her curls gently. 'Nothing happened. Poor child. Something should have happened. Something wonderful.'

'Yes,' she said, almost whispering. 'There was always that emptiness, as if you knew something hadn't happened. Do you know what I mean? It never had a name or a description, it was just—an emptiness.'

'I guess I don't.' His mouth was at her ear, and his warm breath tickled at its lobe. He leaned over her and took the coffee-cup from her hand, setting it down on the coffee-table beside her chair. She felt a curious breathlessness. His hands fumbled for hers, and he gently tugged her up to her feet, facing him.

Peggy took a half step in his direction, and her nose came up against the second button of his shirt. She turned her head and laid her cheek in place against his breastbone—and the world and its atmosphere changed. The magic of the night was still there, but faded into the distance. The grand chorus of the peeper frogs which had haunted them all night became but a note in the darkness. Something—some tension—had come up between them, and she could not tell what it was.

'Peggy?' Just her name, soft and sure and safe.

Yes? was what she had meant to say. 'Yes,' was what she said. His arms came around her, closing her in, just where she wanted to be. For a moment they stood there, locked in an embrace, both his hands at her back. And then his right hand began to move. It drew little circles in the middle of her back, dropped down to her hip, and caressed the fullness there. Another pause.

'Peggy?' he asked.

'Oh, yes,' she sighed. He crushed her to him, so close that she could feel the tightened muscles, the powerful determination. His hand deserted her hip and came round to cup her breast. Peggy moaned at the delight of it as she strained to be closer. Caught up in a web of experience she had never known before, totally relaxed, totally willing, she ached to breathe and could not draw a breath.

'Oh, hell,' he muttered, and swung her up in his arms and carried her back into the house. He hesitated in the middle of the living-room, then turned down the hall and kicked open the door of the nearest bedroom. It had been her mother's, not used since those happier days, but Peggy was not thinking. Her mind was too full of lightning to recognise places. When she felt the mattress surround and accept her she gave one little giggle, and stretched out like an abandoned rag doll.

His hands were busier, and her mind could not measure the reason. There was a coolness as her blouse disappeared, but his warmth overwhelmed her. One thought penetrated. He surely knows how to undress a female! The idea seemed to be so hilarious that she giggled again. Free of all constraints, looking forward to an adventure she had never faced, she rolled over on her back, and then moaned a complaint as his warmth drew away from her.

He was back quickly. Equally naked, her enquiring fingers told her. Equally naked, and sharing the wide bed with her. Her hands reached out to pull him closer. He came, the weight of his head on her breast, his tongue encouraging the proud nipple, his hand wandering. Every touch was fire. She moaned, not knowing what she wanted next, until, after minutes of torture, he took her with him up to where her body was the fuse, her mind the explosion.

When he took her, there was a second of pain and a million years of storm. She clung to him madly throughout the wild ride, drawing blood-lines on his shoulders with her fingernails, shouting her triumph as his weight came down on her and was still, and then lay there gasping, wondering, remembering. 'Oh, God,' she muttered, filled with awe.

'Oh, God—right!' he snapped as he rolled off her and sat on the side of the bed, his back to her.

'What—what's the matter,' she stammered. She reached out to touch him, but he shook her off.

'Why didn't you tell me?' he grated. She could feel his anger, and a cloud of fear struck her.

'You—didn't like it?' How could that be? Nothing could have been so wonderful, nothing. How could he not have liked it?

'I'm not accustomed to doing one-night stands with virgins,' he muttered. 'Where the hell are my——'

A match glowed in the darkness, and Peggy could smell cigarette smoke. But in all the time she had known him he had never smoked!

'What is it?' she asked. 'What's the matter?'

'What's the matter?' he snarled. 'A twenty-six-year-old virgin? What kind of a game is this?' It was a tone she had not heard from him before. He almost seemed to be—afraid.

'I—didn't know it was to be a game,' she sighed. 'It—took me by surprise.'

'Damn! Damn! Damn!' The bed creaked as he stood up. She could hear the dull thud as he beat one fist into the palm of his other hand. 'Well, it's lucky I took precautions,' he muttered, and then flared up in anger. 'I don't suppose *you* would have thought of that?'

'Well, it wasn't as if I had planned it all out,' she snapped, working up to a little anger on her own. 'You know, not all women spend all their time trying to get some man into their bed! But I'm glad you took some precautions. I would certainly hate to think that you'd have to marry me!'

'Marry you? Good lord!' His mind was still whirling, and he didn't like it. Dozens of women, he thought, and I never lost control. Never! And it took her by surprise? Come on now, lady. You've been tempting me all day, and now that I've bitten the apple—hell, she doesn't want a cheque for her bloody arrowroot. Somehow or other she's learned about my bank account. She wants it all! Marry her? He stamped up and down the room, his bare feet making no noise on the polished floor as his mind raked up all the reasons why this—fiasco—had to be all *her* fault. It wasn't hard. He had dodged a dozen man-traps, and knew just how to raise his defences. This scrawny little country girl. Marry her? Good God, what impudence the woman has!

'There was never any thought of marriage,' he told her coldly. 'It was never in the cards. I don't go around committing matrimony with some little backwoods kid.'

'I see.'

He could tell how angry she was. For a second he felt the urge to go back to the bed, to soothe her, to tell her that he really wouldn't mind marrying her! But the thought ran away with him.

'I see,' she repeated. 'This is all part of the service, I suppose. Sell the arrowroot, bed the girl, and go merrily on your way? What did you call it, a one-night stand?'

'That's it exactly,' he growled as he fumbled for his clothes, ignoring the clamour in his heart.

'And I suppose that the bedding is your payment for your altruistic little act, Mr Marston.' He could mark the change in her voice. First, a spirit of wonder, then a touch of anger, and now the words dripped with venom.

'Exactly. You hit the nail right on the head,' he muttered. 'And don't think it was any great prize. I never knew a virgin to turn in an outstanding performance in bed. It takes practice.'

'I'm sure it does,' she said bitterly. 'I only wish I could have the opportunity to take more lessons from you. I wouldn't want to be caught short the next time.'

'That could be arranged,' he snapped. 'See my secretary and make an appointment.'

'I don't think I'd want to stand in line, even with a man like you,' she said softly.

His conscience drove him. 'Look, I'm sorry——'

'Don't be,' she chided him gently. She sat up, pulling her knees up to her breasts, feeling the cold shudder run up and down her spine, none of it engendered by the warm tropical night. 'Please—don't say you're sorry. Not now. That would be the ultimate insult. It had to happen sometime. It does to every woman. And, in a way, I'm glad it was you. But I think——' Her voice broke as the tears began to fall. 'I think you had better leave, Mr Marston. I don't want to see your face again!'

'You'll see it,' he threatened. 'In the morning, when you're more calm. We have a few things to wrap up on this deal. And then I'll arrange for you to have your wish. I only came here to do you a favour, lady. I suppose this is what happens when a guy tries some do-gooding. Don't, for God's sake, make a mountain out of it. You're not the first woman ever to get laid on a balmy night. But I am surprised you waited so many years for it to happen!'

He managed to find his way out of the door, just in time. The lamp by the bed crashed into the wall inches from his head as he went. And that's gratitude for you, he thought, as he pounded down the hall. I came up here strictly on a mission of goodwill. Out of the damned kindness of my heart I've worked to seal a deal for her. And she wanted it all, damn her. The deal, the excitement, the bedding. All I did was oblige! Marriage! He shuddered as he went into his own room and slammed the door behind him. But, although he worked hard on his self-justification, it was barely enough to overcome the sound of sobs that echoed down the hall.

He lay in bed for about half an hour, when he heard the patter of her bare feet going down the hall to her own bedroom. Silence closed in on the house, but Jim was unable to sleep. He tossed and turned, counted moonbeams, and thought, I came on a vacation trip, and met the little damsel in distress purely by accident. Ordinarily I would have run the minute I heard her story, or, at the most, recommended a good lawyer. But no, I'm the good guy in this little plot. I go a long way out of my path to rig a deal for her. The deal is perfectly honest. So we play around a little bit. Why not? And she gives me those come-on smiles every time I turn around. What's to lose? At her age she surely knows the score. Why shouldn't we top it off with a little bedroom pool? So where did it go wrong?

You know where it went wrong, his heart told him. It went wrong the day you fell in love with her, fool! Remember, sitting up there with your feet dangling over the edge at Sunset Point, watching the night creep in? So what happened to the Wall Street wolf, the man who had been in love with women a thousand times before? Why was it that none of those times were the same as this? Damn it, Marston, shake yourself out of this foolishness. Be logical. You both wanted it tonight. She enjoyed it, as you did, too. Nobody's at fault.

His little argument seemed to make sense. But imposed on his logic was the remembrance of her sitting up in bed, those big green eyes of hers shadowed and puzzled and pained. At two o'clock in the morning he rolled out of the bed, slipped quietly into his clothes, and walked out of the door. He took two steps down the corridor towards the porch door, then stopped and back-tracked. Peggy's room was the last one in the north wing of the house.

Jim Marston was a big man, but capable of quiet movement. He slipped off his shoes and went noiselessly in the other direction. The bedroom door at the end of the hall was ajar. Cautiously he used a finger to push it back. Peggy was asleep, sprawled out on her back in a long cotton nightgown, clutching her pillow in her arms. The moon was bright, almost as bright as daylight. She had one hand over her eyes, but he could see the tear-streaks down her cheeks, and occasionally she would moan and her body would jerk as if in pain. His heart seemed to jump a beat, but his self-righteous will-power pulled him away.

Dear God, what's the matter with me? He moved over to the bed and gently touched the carving on the headboard. The room shrieked at him, the room and all the memories. Marston snatched the finger back as if he were a thief trapped in the night. As he backed out of the room he could feel an unusual thing. Those were tears forming in his own eyes.

Back in the corridor again, he turned round and looked again, but did not re-enter. Almost he wanted to wake her, but as he thought about it the girl whimpered in her sleep and rolled over, turning her back to him. It was as if she had slammed a door in his face. He shook his head and walked out of the house.

Pepper came up and nosed at him as he sat down on the bottom porch-step to put his shoes back on, and the dog followed him for a few paces down the moonlit path, but then turned back. A couple of times he tripped on unseen roots, but he ploughed ahead until he reached the track. There was only one bus this far out, he knew, and it came at nine in the morning. But there was another alternative. Châteaubelair was less than four miles away, hardly a long walk in the cool of the pre-dawn. And from Châteaubelair motor launches travelled to Kingstown irregularly.

He arrived at the dock in the pre-dawn. The moon had long since set in the far reaches of the Caribbean, but General Stonewall Jackson's adage still applied. It was daylight whenever a man could see his hand held twelve inches in front of his face! And from then on everything was simplified. There was only one dock. Tied up to it was only one launch. The captain was prepared to leave for the capital at nine in the morning. Influenced by fifty American dollars, he cast off in fifteen minutes. As the boat swung out into the sea to achieve seaway for Layou Point, Jim kept watch astern, where the looming bulk of Mt Soufrière marked the site of the Mitchell plantation on its flank. He continued to look, even as the launch turned the point and headed south-eastward towards Kingstown and the Bequia channel.

There was another advantage. The waterfront at Kingstown was absolutely still, and the launch ran him up alongside *Sea-Witch*, his own yacht. In another hour he was cleared for sailing, and the gleaming mainsail of the boat was filling as he headed for the Atlantic side of St Vincent and turned north, heading for St Lucia.

With the sail drawing well in a following wind, the auto-pilot locked in, and a mug of instant coffee cradled in his hand, he did one more thing. He turned on his radio-telephone and made contact with a sleepy marine telephone operator back in Kingstown.

The voice of his principal aide in New York was about as unpleasant as one would expect of someone being called at six o'clock in the morning, but he stamped out the grumbling with an ungracious 'Shut up and listen.' And the young man, who had earned more than a little money while following his boss's tips, did just that.

'I want,' Jim Marston said in his most demanding voice, 'two things. First, I want you to buy me five hundred sweet almond saplings, and ship them by air to Miss Margarita Mitchell, on St Vincent Island in the Grenadines.'

'By air? That'll cost a fortune, sir.'

'Just do it, Murphy. And be damn quick about it.'

'Yes, sir. And this other thing?'

'Find me some damn law office in Chicago by the name of Simon & Poke, and find out everything you can about the estate of a man named Brennan. Patrick Brennan, I believe the name is. I believe I know the location of his only granddaughter. And, Murphy—call them *now*. I want to hear from you within twenty-four hours!'

Flipping off the switch of the radio set made him feel a little better, although he could not, for the life of him, understand why he should feel so guilty about all that had happened. The hell you can't! his conscience shouted at him.

Peggy Mitchell slept late. When she burrowed her way out on to the floor she could hear a clatter in the kitchen, and Bea's calm voice as she sang her favourite song, 'Amazing Grace'. Peggy looked glumly out of the window at the sun-shadow. So the world *hasn't* come to an end, she told herself bitterly. And I suppose he was right. I'm not the only woman who was... She pushed the words and the picture away from her, and ran for the bathroom.

Cold showers did wonders for a girl, she knew. Either they froze the outside of you to match the temperature of your heart, or they threw you back out of your stupid dreams into the real world! Peggy fell into the latter class. He had said he would be around in the morning, so she had that to face! She struggled back to her bedroom, dressed sensibly in an old cotton shift, brushed her hair carelessly, and went out to the kitchen.

Bea was standing at the kitchen stove, and turned round as Peggy came in. 'I glad I come home early,' the housekeeper said complacently. 'You make an awful mess in the kitchen last night, missy. I don't know you can cook like that. I sample everything!'

'Oh, Bea,' Peggy returned, 'I'm so glad you're back. And no, I didn't cook all that. Mr Marston did. Where is he?'

'Don't taste like no man made all that,' Bea chuckled. 'No man that smart.'

'Well maybe Ada Coeurdeleon helped,' Peggy added. 'Mr Marston? Where is he?'

'Gone, missy. Everything cleared up in his room, and he gone. I come up the trail by seven o'clock. He must have go very early.'

'Oh, lord,' Peggy sighed. 'I—wanted to say something to him.'

'He be back,' the old woman promised. 'I read the cards, missy. He be back some day soon.'

'No, I don't think so,' Peggy murmured. And he was right. It was all my fault. I wanted it as badly as he did. I was as greedy as anyone he ever knew, and then to throw myself at him, to seduce him like that. I should have explained. But—now it's too late! She stabbed a thumb at her bleary eyes and sat down at the breakfast table.

'I won't forget him,' she whispered.

'What you say?' Bea carried the frying-pan to the draining-board, and smiled at her chick.

'Nothing,' Peggy sighed. 'I was thinking about last night. You know, that Vera Helst came and brought the cheque. They bought everything we had, Bea!'

'Jus' so they didn't buy you to go with it,' Bea announced. 'I gonna go strip all the beds. Funny, I go away jus' three-four days and everything gets in the wrong places and covered with dust and dirt!'

'I suppose it's because we don't have your neat genes,' Peggy tossed after her. It was hard to be humorous, with all the misery piled up in her mind. But that was something she had to work her way out of! A cup of cold tea sat on the table in front of her. She picked it up and sipped—and suddenly the kitchen door slammed back.

'Missy!' Bea roared, her face lit in anger. Peggy's cup spilled over before she could ground it. 'How could you!'

'Could I what?' she asked nervously.

'What you think, I am born tomorrow?' Bea was undoubtedly angry, overwhelmingly so. In her hands were a pair of rumpled sheets. 'I tell you an' tell you all these years. I tell him, too. Keep you hands in you pockets, man, I say to him. And look!' she waved the sheets in front of her as if they were evidence in a murder case. 'An' in you mama's bed, too. Margarita Mitchell, ain't you got no shame!'

Peggy blinked her eyes, but refused to cry. 'I've got plenty of that, Bea,' she said mournfully. 'More than enough. But yelling at me isn't going to help. That's one step which you can't back off from.'

Bea dropped the sheets and rushed round the table to comfort her. 'Me an' my big mouth,' the old lady said.

'Hey, now. You right, love. Can't turn back from this. What he say?'

'Not much,' Peggy replied. 'Practically nothing before—and, as I recall, all he said afterwards was goodbye! It wasn't what I would call an outstanding performance by either of us. And it was really all my fault. I never thought it would happen that way!'

'Not to worry,' Bea comforted. 'You like this man?'

'I—yes, I liked him, Bea. But he's gone, right? End of chapter. Time to turn the next page and get on with my life.'

'You probably right, missy,' the old black woman agreed. 'We jus' go ahead. Only you remember: in good stories sometimes the same man keeps appearin' in all them chapters! Now, you go get yourself cleaned up.'

Peggy went back to the bathroom and took another cold shower. And then, because she had showered with enthusiasm, the bathroom needed considerable cleaning up afterwards. Peggy was in the middle of all this when Bea bustled excitedly into the room behind her.

'Missy,' she exclaimed, holding one hand behind her back. Peggy, who was down on hands and knees using a bath towel to dry the floor, came to her feet with a groan.

'What now, Bea? The world is really coming to an end?'

'I don' know about that part,' the housekeeper said, 'but I don't do a very good job in you mama's room—until today. An' underneath her mattress, look what I found!'

The envelope she held in her hand was addressed in Peggy's mother's wavering hand, but it was clear enough. 'Simon & Poke', it said, and the address was in downtown Chicago.

'I don't understand,' Peggy wailed. 'What——'

'The letter you mother wrote,' Bea said. 'Send it the day I die, that what she said, missy. I think you mailed it.'

'And I thought *you* mailed it,' Peggy moaned. 'Oh, lord, and it never *did* get in the mail! So the lawyers have no idea about us! All those months we've wasted, waiting.'

'Work of the Lord,' Bea announced in her most solemn voice. 'He don' want that letter delivered. Of course not. He want sumpin' else for my missy. What I tell you! I read it all in the cards!'

'I—just don't understand.' Peggy Mitchell was already lost in another torment. So much of her hope had been pinned on Jim Marston, and he had fulfilled all his promises, *before she told him to go away*! And before that so much of her courage had depended upon the day when they would hear from Simon & Poke. And *they* knew no more about her than Jim did! Like a marion-ette whose strings had been cut, Peggy collapsed against the side of the shower-stall, her eyes big with unstated fears. '*Everything* was the truth,' she sighed. 'Every-thing. He told me the truth, asked for my trust, and I turned him out of the house as if he were a bandit. Oh, my God!'

Bea looked at the girl, leaning there in a state of shock, and for once her own faith in the Tarot was diminished. 'Poor missy,' she comforted, pulling the girl's head over to rest on her massive bosom. 'Sometimes women make fool mistakes about men.'

# CHAPTER NINE

THERE was a peculiarity to life, Peggy found. Even in the gloomiest of times it insisted on going on. Bea still bustled around the house, smiling. In the wake of her progress, Peggy, deep in depression, was drawn along, aware there was no way she could avoid Bea and Henry. But, on the day following that on which Bea's arms had comforted her, she threw off the despondency. Things were not exactly the way they had been when her mother had died. That epic crossing had been a relief—a thankfulness that her beloved mother had crossed over into a better land, where her pains were stilled and her goodness rewarded. Peggy had *worked* her way out of that time, and would do so again, she promised herself grimly.

So, that day, she went out of the house into the sunshine. From the nearest fields she could hear the sound of voices singing and arguing. She walked in that direction.

'Got mos' everybody in the village,' Henry reported with a grin. 'Men, women, children. We gonna have this crop out by the end of the day, missy.'

'They paid you in advance, Henry?'

'Better b'lieve.' He shifted his weight, resting one foot on the heel of his spade. After all, Peggy thought, he's a grandfather many times over! The land remains the same, but the people grow older. Too bad not all of us grow smarter in the doing! 'I remember what you said,' the amiable giant continued. 'Certified cheque in advance, hey? What's good enough for missy, good enough for us. Go down to bank pretty soon, me, and change it for real money.'

And that's what I ought to do, Peggy told herself. You had the word from the biggest con-man of them all. It's only the money that counts! 'I'm going today,' she said, deciding as she stood there. 'As soon as I can!'

'You miss the nine o'clock bus,' Henry pointed out. 'Already nine-fifteen.'

'I don't know how you do that without a watch,' Peggy said sadly, 'but you're always right, Henry. Well, I'll walk into Châteaubelair and take a launch.'

'No rule says lady mus' stand around house and look gloomy,' Henry agreed. 'I get the paper, you cash our cheque too? You don' mind to do such an errand?'

'I don't mind.' Teased into a laugh, and committed by comment, Peggy accepted the cheque, changed into her second-best dress, the yellow one that covered her from high neck to below the knees, 'An' don' forget you hat,' Bea insisted. 'No sense you get all freckles. Ain't nobody on this island got skin nice like you, missy. That hat, you hear me?'

Feeling like a chastised schoolgirl, Peggy went back into the house for her hat, and gave Bea the hug that had been missing for so long. The housekeeper was not impressed. She was up to her elbows in flour, working on the week's bread supply. 'You need to get outside in the sunshine,' she advised Peg. 'See if you can't find you another man!'

Stripped of her bravado, Peggy turned and fled, her heels clicking like castanets on the bare wood of the corridor.

The dusty walk to Châteaubelair restored her good humour. The launch was a bit behind schedule, three hours or more. Due to the appearance of a pod of dolphins, the captain explained. Naturally he had stopped to watch. And all the passengers agreed that it was the sensible thing to do. All of which put her in Kingstown at noon, just as the bells of both cathedrals began to sound. Her humour was considerably improved as she watched the hordes of pigeons scatter from the sound.

Luckily the bank did not close until one for its siesta. Otherwise she would have been town-captured until six in the evening. She had dealt with the same teller for the past six years.

'Now, you want the harvesting cheque in cash?' Mr Albert asked.

'Small bills,' she agreed. 'We want to pay off all the hands as soon as I can get back.'

'And the sales cheque?'

'I want part of it to pay off the mortgage, and the rest in the current account.'

'Smart move, this certified cheque,' he approved. 'Did you know that a couple of people came in here yesterday and tried to stop payment on this very cheque? Very charming, fast-talkers. Funny they should think that because we live in a small town we think the same way! The president of the bank, he set a flea in their ear, b'lieve me. And by the way, we have notice from your Mr Marston. He asks the bank to serve as his agent. So where do you want them?'

Peggy clutched at the corner of his desk to maintain her equilibrium. 'He is *not my* Mr Marston,' she said slowly but firmly. 'Not at all.' The man opposite her raised his eyebrows at the vehemence. 'And I haven't the slightest idea where I want what,' she finished with a sigh. 'What are you talking about?'

The corner of Mr Albert's mouth went up, which was about all he ever could muster for a smile.

'The trees,' he explained. 'Mr Marston sent you some almond trees. They came in by special chartered cargo plane early this morning.'

'A couple of almond trees?' It brought back happy memories, so vivid that she could almost smell the scent of the blossoms as she smelt it when they had sat in the park that day. So he hadn't forgotten. Her heart clutched at the idea. He hadn't forgotten! 'That's nice,' she told the teller. 'A couple of trees around the house would be nice. Could you have Willie Sutton bring them out in his truck some day?'

Since the customer was always right, Mr Albert beamed at her and nodded. When Peggy went out the door her step was just the slightest bit lighter, her mood a trifle happier, the sun a tiny bit brighter. And behind her the teller struggled with paper and pencil. Five hundred almond trees in the primary order, and one hundred more in case some of the first group didn't survive. And how many trips would it require in Willie Sutton's truck to get them all out to the Mitchell plantation?

'So you looks better for the trip,' Bea muttered as they sat round the early evening dinner table. 'The bonito, they runnin' in the channel. I got plenty fish. You eat, missy.'

'You needn't push, Bea,' Peggy returned softly. 'I'm getting it all behind me——'

'You thinks,' Bea interrupted. 'Eat. A girl never forgets her first man. Not never.'

'Well, this girl will,' Peggy said determinedly. 'This girl will. Tomorrow I'm going after all the weeds in the vegetable garden. And the day after——'

'An' after that the pigsty need cleanin', and the barn in bad shape, and the house fallin' down. But you stubborn, girl. You don't admit nothin', huh? After dinner I gonna read the cards.'

'You know I don't believe in such nonsense,' Peggy spluttered.

'Course not,' Bea replied derisively. 'You got all that education, you don't gonna believe in nothin' like the Tarot. They teach you everything in that nursing school, no?'

'Oh, lordy, Bea, I don't mean anything. Read the cards. It can't help. But——'

'I know, missy. But you don't gotta believe. Go take care of you goats, while I does the dishes and warms up the cards.' Bea's big black eyes followed Peggy as she went out the door. Eyes filled with compassion, love, and more than a modicum of hope. She riffled the Tarot pack in her hands a couple of times, then set it down to get at the dishes.

The goats were particularly obnoxious, at a time when Peg needed soothing. Even Satan refused to be driven into his stall in the barn, and it was not until Pepper, the dog, aided in the herding that the mission was accomplished. Peggy was talking to herself when she finally shut his stall gate and wandered back to the kitchen.

'What you say?' Bea was at the table, the card pack spread out in front of her.

'That donkey,' Peggy said. 'He's getting altogether too big for his breeches. He thinks he owns the farm and that I'm the slave. Well, I'm not going to let him dictate what man I take up with. Or you either, old lady!'

'No, of course not,' Bea hastened to assure her, wondering how she and the donkey had been judged on the same level. 'Not me. Why I have anything to say about your man? Take a card.'

Peggy moved her hand without thinking, and turned over the Sun. Bea looked at it carefully, took control of the pack, and began to lay out the cards, talking softly as she did so. The words poured over Peggy's head, but her mind was lost in thought. The sun. Symbol of a creative life, a good marriage, achievement. Followed by the Empress, to question whether or not she had the power to find those goals. And the Hanged Man, signifying willing self-sacrifice. Peggy barely heard the rest of the reading.

As she handled the cards, feeling the vibrant life in them through her old fingers, Bea talked on, one eye on the pasteboards as they fell, the other on the dreaming girl. With a start, the old woman paused. They had gone through the cards of the past and the present, and now were following the path of the future. Almost as if they were an identity, the cards were laying out the same path she had read for Jim Marston. Heartbreak, darkness, fire and danger, travel over water—Bea held her breath as she turned over the last card, and then sighed with relief. The Lovers, in their positive aspect!

The old woman laid the last card down gently. The Lovers. Final achievement. Love uncontaminated by material desires. She sat there quietly, her forefinger in the centre of the card, her eyes on the girl who sat opposite her, dreaming.

True to her vow, Peggy was out in the vegetable patch the next morning, just after sunrise. Bea followed her out, intending to get some outdoor air for herself. 'You hat,' the old woman said threateningly. 'You want you should be all freckles and sunburn? What kind of way is that to get a man?'

'I don't want a man,' Peggy grumbled as she chopped vigorously at the weeds which tried to hide under a row of cabbages. 'Who needs a man when I've got you and all these fine vegetables?'

'Keep you feet off the tomato vines,' Bea advised, 'an'
maybe we get by. They ain't as useful as a man,
but——' With which she tramped off, back into her own
domain, the kitchen.

The day passed quickly. Hard work was a panacea for
*something*, but for what Peggy was not quite sure. That
fool man's face kept getting in the way of her eyesight.
Satan the donkey had come over to help her weed, and
wasn't doing too well at it. His idea of weeding a garden
was to sit down in the middle of it and pull up everything that showed green. He kept at it until a parade of
little red ants crossed his path, doing their own nef-
arious bit. Satan was no dullard. Those were fire ants.
He scrambled to his four feet, brayed an alarm, and
stalked off to better pastures.

They all went to bed early, but sleep came late for
Peggy. Because of your tired muscles, she told herself.
And it might well have been just that. The next day there
was the barn to be cleaned, but more slowly. The strained
muscles had not yielded to the home-prescription lotion
that Bea produced. And the following day the pigsty,
and the following the chicken run. That was the day when
all the labourers, having completed the harvesting of the
arrowroot, piled it all on the trucks, and went back to
the village to celebrate. They invited Peggy to join them,
but her back was bothering her, so she offered her regrets.

And the next morning, when she got up at the usual
time, the sun was not shining. A simple statement, that,
and probably not unusual at all in northern climes, but
in the tropics on St Vincent the sun was *always* shining.
Oh, there were moments when clouds covered everything, everywhere, as they always did on the top of Mt
Soufrière. And in the hurricane season storms would
cover the world from horizon to horizon for a time. But,
beyond that, there was sunshine. Even in the middle of

a rainstorm one could see the edges of the storm, and the sunbeams that sparkled at its limits. So this morning was different.

'Trouble,' Bea said gloomily as Peggy hurried out into the kitchen. 'Feel that? Somethin' shake the house. Big troubles. They a big cloud on top the mountain!'

'They always a big cloud on top the mountain,' Peggy protested, slipping into the dialect.

'Not like this here cloud,' Bea insisted. 'Go, look.'

Peggy went out to the back porch to see. High over her head, where normally rain-clouds surrounded the truncated cone of the old mountain, there was indeed a different sort of cloud. And as she stood there assessing it, an explosion somewhere high on the mountainside shook the whole valley, and a plume of steam shot high in the air. Not at the mountain-top, but rather from some vent slightly lower on the west side of the barren crag. And then, having made its noisy protest and shown its displeasure, the mountain brought the action to a halt. Peggy ducked back into the house and searched out the battery transistor radio.

'Something on the mountain,' she called to Bea as she went by the kitchen door. 'But it stopped.'

'Ain't no fool mountain make a little gulp like that,' Bea yelled after her. 'You don't remember 1979, hey? That mountain have a bad dream, he hiccup, we in a lot of trouble, missy.'

'Don't be a gloom-and-doom sayer,' Peggy said as she brought the radio into the kitchen. 'Nothing's going to happen to the mountain!' *I hope*, she told herself fiercely. I hope nothing's going to happen to the mountain. But the short hairs at the back of her neck were standing straight up. The ground had stirred twice more since she had come back into the house. Trying to reassure Bea,

Peg Mitchell was fighting off the fingers of fear that reached out to her.

'Lot you know,' Bea mumbled as she went about the breakfast routine. 'Before my time, 1902, ole man mountain blow the top off, burn everything down like crazy, raise plenty hell. 1979 he blow the top again, huh? Don't burn much, but ruin all the crop, scare everybody. Me, I scare easy!'

'So do I,' Peggy muttered to herself as she twisted the knob of the radio and finally picked up the station in Kingstown. Music flooded the room; a calypso band, offering the sprightly music of the steel drums. And then came a change.

'We interrupt our programme for this announcement. The Governor-General and the Prime Minister caution all residents of the northern end of the island that Mt Soufrière is in the preliminary stages of a possible eruption. All residents on the east coast, from Fancy to Orange Hill, are requested to evacuate the area as quickly as possible. Buses are now being sent up both the Windward and the Leeward Highways to help in the evacuation. Residents of the farm areas on the Caribbean side, north of Châteaubelair, are cautioned to evacuate with the utmost speed. Residents south of the line running from Châteaubelair to Georgetown, on both coasts, are warned to make preparations for further evacuations. This is not a practice! The Governor-General asks also that families living in the south of the island be prepared to assist the evacuees. This is not a practice. Mt Soufrière——' The announcer's voice broke off for a moment, and background talk could be heard over the microphone before the man returned, and took up where he had left off, but with considerably less aplomb. 'Mt Soufrière is definitely erupting!' he half-shouted.

'Oh, God,' Peggy muttered as she turned the knob off. 'Bea, they don't have a radio in the village. You go down and warn them. I'll pack a few things and come down as soon as I turn the animals loose from the barn. Tell them all to head for Châteaubelair. If they don't find the buses or the launches at 'belair, then keep walking south!'

'Don't need no packin',' the old woman declared. 'Jus' need runnin'!'

'Well, start,' Peggy demanded. 'Start *now*! I've got to get the animals out!' Taking a quick look out the window as Bea hustled down the path, Peggy saw the snow. Little fluttering white specks, too far south to *really* be snow. She stepped out on the porch for a closer look. Ash, white-hot ash, blowing up out of the new vent in the mountainside, and then falling like a snowstorm across the base of the mountain. A wind out of the north-east was spreading it far and fast. And intermingled here and there within the ash-storm were tiny bits of burning substance, sparkling red against the black sky and the white storm. The hounds began to bay. Old Pepper limped round the corner of the house and sat at Peggy's foot, nestling as close as he could squeeze.

St Lucia lay some twenty miles north of St Vincent, its tropical, mountainous beauty attracting a booming tourist industry.

Jim Marston had not pushed *Sea-Witch* but, under the force of a following wind, he brought the gleaming white yacht in through the narrow entrance to Castries Harbour in something under record time. At the direction of a pilot, he took the boat almost a mile inland, although not by any means to the end of the long narrow harbour. Above his head was the hilltop called Morne Fortune, once a major French fort over which Queen Victoria's father had hoisted the British colours in 1794, while the Inniskilling Fusiliers celebrated the victory.

But Marston was in no mood to celebrate. Throughout the sea trip he had paid little attention to navigation. Instead, he concentrated on the few days he had spent on the Mitchell plantation. And despite his self-righteous defences, he knew, as he approached Castries, that he had made a monumental mistake. The attraction that he felt for Peggy was not some casual affection. He *loved* the girl. And like some fool from the back country he had seduced her, insulted her, and sailed away. Bluebeard the pirate couldn't have done it better! So when his hook dropped into the soft bottom of St Lucia's major harbour he did the only thing possible. He called a bum-boat, arranged for it to bring him a case of the best Scotch whisky in town, and proceeded to get thoroughly and miserably drunk.

He came up for air on the next day, managed to feed himself, shower and shave, and checked in by radio-telephone with his New York office.

'Yes, sir,' Frank Murphy told him. 'The trees have been shipped. Yes sir, by air. We had to charter a plane, but—yes, sir, that's what I told our comptroller, sir. And on that other matter, sir. Yes. I contacted Simon & Poke. They were glad to hear from you. It seems that your Mr Brennan had left his daughter—and, I suppose, his granddaughter—a small legacy. About nine thousand dollars, sir. What? Jump through my—that's physically impossible to—yes, sir. Goodbye—sir.'

Giving someone else a hard time left Jim Marston feeling the slightest bit better. Her grandfather had left her nine thousand dollars? A slip of the decimal point could make that ninety thousand, and be a good reason for him to go back to St Vincent. Not a reason, but a hell of a good excuse, his conscience nagged. She would see through it too easily, and demand an accounting, and the whole thing would blow up in my face!

Ordinarily a man of Jim's decisiveness would have come up with half a dozen alternatives, selected the best of them, and gone about a solution. But *this* problem involved a face that haunted him, a pair of green twinkling eyes, the most ridiculous red hair in the world. And how, in God's name, having so grossly insulted her, did you wheel up in your fancy yacht and say, 'Margarita Mitchell, I love you'? No, that was certainly not the way. So he went back to the bottle again.

Several days later, when he surfaced, he knew something was wrong. There was an electric feeling throughout the harbour. Everyone he came across seemed to be waiting for something to happen. And when he had finally cleaned himself up well enough to ask the harbourmaster, that worthy merely waved his hand towards the south. 'There,' he said.

Jim swivelled around. From Castries the view was blocked to the southward by mountains. But there was something to see. A puff of darkness was zooming up beyond the five-thousand-foot altitude, and the muffled sound of an explosion could be heard.

'Soufrière,' the harbourmaster commented casually, using the stem of his pipe as a pointer. 'The mountain, not the town. It's been struggling to blow ever since dawn. There'll be hell to pay all along the north coast of St Vincent. Was here in 1979, I was, when the same thing——' The old man stopped talking. He had lost his audience.

Jim ran the fifty yards at almost Olympic speed to the slip where he had temporarily moored *Sea-Witch*. He made no effort to raise the mainsail. The usual trade winds would be off his port bow when he hit the open ocean, and he had no time for tacking back and forth. Instead he kicked in the two inboard diesel engines, and came out of Castries harbour at eleven knots, throwing up a wake that rocked half the moored pleasure craft in the harbour, and almost sank a flat-bottomed rowing-boat.

*Sea-Witch* moved out into her own element, swaying in concert with the moody Caribbean, plunging ahead with spume flaring over the decks. Jim Marston stood at the wheel aft, cursing himself, the weather, the wind, the world, pounding on the steering equipment, searching for every possible bit of extra power.

Ahead of him St Vincent rose up out of the ocean. He could see the line of sunshine that lit the island south of Châteaubelair. Everything to the north was in darkness. The first drift of ash had settled. More was falling, but mixed in with it were burning embers. Already dry patches in the rain forest, on the mountain's flank, were ablaze. Coming closer, he could see one or two flimsy cane huts on fire. There was a muted roar in his ears, and the little harbour at Châteaubelair was just too far away.

He riffled through the collection of charts and located a nearer landing. Wallilabou River, that icy stream which flowed directly down the flank of the mountain, and formed the beach where the two of them, Peggy and he, had spent so pleasant a day—a day that seemed years ago.

River was a misnomer for the Wallilabou. It was a mountain freshet, and the charts showed an extremely narrow channel through the reefs. Nothing was more dangerous than for one man to take a boat into an area of known and unknown reefs by himself. With no lookouts, no warnings, only sheer luck could have brought him safely to the shore. But Marston was not

a man to quibble with luck. He pushed as fast and as
far as he could at full speed, until his charts and his
fathometer indicated shoaling water, with less than a
fathom under his keel. Only then did he throttle back,
watching in the semi-darkness for the poorly defined line
where cold fresh water was forcing its way out into the
warm salt sea.

With little more than headway he prodded and probed
at the land, inching forward. The smoke, the ash, the
embers were all around him. Ashore he could see practically nothing. He flipped on his commercial radio, and
tuned to the Kingstown station, just in time to hear the
announcer say, 'The two bridges near Châteaubelair have
been blocked by fire and falling timber. Any residents
still in the area are urged to go to the sea and wait. Keep
low, below the smoke level. It is the smoke that kills!
Rescue is coming!'

'You're damned well right,' Jim muttered. Just at that
moment a gust of wind blew a hole in the curtain of
smoke and ash, and there, directly in front of him, was
the long beach where the boys had played cricket. With
a shouted curse he shut his engines and ran forward,
managing barely to drop the anchor before the yacht ran
aground.

There were figures on the beach ahead of him. Not
many, but a few. They waved in desperation, but their
voices were drowned out as the mountain roared again
over the heads, and moments later the falling ash re-
doubled. The yacht was the only escape route. To be
sure of that route Marston, against the drive of his heart,
delayed long enough to drop a second anchor aft, and
to use a canvas pail to soak the decks and rigging of
*Sea-Witch*.

The ten-minute delay was more than his mind could
stand. Somewhere on that beach, on that hill, in those

clouds, Peggy Mitchell might be standing—might be dying. He roared against the futility of it all as he threw the rubber dinghy over the side and paddled swiftly ashore. An ember fell on his back. He shook it off before the burn became too severe. When he grounded the dinghy there were several pairs of hands waiting to help pull it up on the beach.

Six people, he counted. Three children, one man, two women. One of the women was Bea. And the man, thank God, was Henry Coeurdeleon.

'Henry,' he yelled. 'Get them all out to the yacht. Keeping dousing the deck and sails with water. If things look too bad, leave.'

'An' how about you?' the big man asked.

'I have to find Miss Peggy!' he yelled.

'She still up on the mountain,' Bea screamed at him. 'She say you go ahead, warn the village. I don't go more than two hundred feet, maybe less, and the fire break out behind me. I don' know how she get through. All those animals locked in the barn. She wouldn't leave them there. Oh, lordy, my poor baby!'

'We get everyone else out by the road,' Henry added. 'Only us left.' The other woman turned out to be Ada who, while the men were talking, had ushered the children into the boat. They huddled there, eyes wide with fear, while Ada turned to comfort Bea.

'You gonna go, I go with you,' Henry said. Jim shook his head.

'You take these people out to the boat,' he insisted. 'There's no way they could handle things by themselves. I'm going after Peggy. If you have to leave, don't worry. We'll survive somehow.'

'You don' gotta go,' Henry yelled at him.

'Yes, I do!' he yelled back. 'It's all my fault!'

The little cortège of people watched him soak his shirt and trousers in sea-water and then disappear up the trail.

'Crazy,' Henry muttered as he pushed the rubber boat back off the beach. 'All his fault? Ole man mountain blow he top, and it is all his fault?'

'You don' understand,' his wife assured him as she helped him into the boat. 'You too old, man. You got strength for to paddle?'

'I got strength to paddle,' Henry Coeurdeleon announced. 'Paddle boat an' you too, woman, you don' hush you mouth!'

The first few feet up the path were no problem. Jim went as fast as his eyes could discern the way. But by the time he reached the level of the village he had been burned half a dozen times, his shirt was in tatters, and the rest of him was covered in grey ash.

He stopped in the village street, stretching out in the narrow ruts to get a deep breath, and to avoid the smoke. But something was driving him. Ahead there was nothing recognisable. Flame and fire and smoke had obliterated the familiar landmarks. All he could be sure of was that he had to go *up*! So he plunged recklessly ahead, making a path where none had existed before.

Twice his way was blocked by a wall of fire. In each case he managed to snatch banana leaves off wild plants, and used the fronds to beat a path through. He was no longer running now. Bent almost double to keep below the level of the smoke, he had torn off his shirt and wrapped its rags around his nose and mouth. But still his feet carried him inexorably upward. A drum was beating in his mind. A drum and a battle cry. Peggy, Peggy, Peggy, the beat said.

So much was he concentrating that when his foot caught in the trailing vine he dived head first into the ashy heap in front of him, and came up on one knee, considerably battered. The smoke was swamping lower and lower.

'Peggy,' he bellowed desperately. 'Peggy!' The yell was almost enough to override the steady roar that came from the volcano, and it was successful.

A small body, dressed in ash and soot and a torn skirt, came hurtling out of the bush above him, screaming, and smashed into him at the knees hard enough to knock him over. His hand moved without thought, snatching her up against him. 'Peggy,' he muttered in her ear. 'Peggy!'

She stopped screaming, but was obviously on the edge of hysteria. 'Jim,' she croaked painfully. 'Jim—oh, God, Jim! How could it be you? I must be——'

Jim Marston sat down and gathered her into his arms. She collapsed, resting her head on his shoulder. Her body was shaking uncontrollably. In some way, Jim knew, he had to stop the hysteria, or they would never be able to make their way down the hill again. Trying to make his voice as casual as possible, he said, 'Lord, I've always hated watering pots. Everything is all right, and I love you.'

'What?' Her head came up off his shoulder. 'Why, you rotten——' she started to say, and then her mind went into first gear.

'And I love you,' he repeated. She leaned against him, her mouth half open, unable to find the words. 'I had to come back,' he went on casually. 'I left my wrist-watch behind, and I want to marry you.'

'Jim——' she muttered, and then caught the other operative words. 'Marry you?' Her hand reached out and touched his face gently, feeling all the crags and indentations. 'Marry you?' she repeated, dazed.

'Marry me,' he said firmly. 'And pretty quick, too.'

'But I——' Her voice cracked. 'You crazy fool,' she berated him. 'You came all the way up here to find me? You could have been killed. And then what would I do? And I don't know where your darn wristwatch is because the house burned down to the ground, and—Marry you?'

'Marry me,' he repeated. 'And if you don't I'm going to stay right here and cry and eat dirt.'

'You're crazy,' she sighed, and then her fingers traced the corner of his cheek. 'You get a girl in a corner and then you threaten marriage! And you need a shave.'

'OK,' he teased. 'OK. I'm no hard-head. I'm willing to compromise. If I shave, will you marry me?'

'Oh, Jim,' she cried, and threw herself against his shoulder. He supported her head with one hand, and let her cry it out. In a moment she sniffled back the remaining tears. 'I look a fright, don't I? I know what you're trying to do. You're trying to shake me out of the screaming meemies, aren't you? Well, it worked. Shall we start down?'

'I never saw anyone more beautiful,' he said honestly. 'But it's getting late, and lunch is being served down at the beach. Will you?'

'Will I what? Eat lunch with you?' Her mind was still whirling. The fire had frightened her completely beyond her strength to resist. And now this—man—who had stormed off in the night, running at the very mention of the word marriage, was sitting there under the smoke cloud and using that same word as if it were peanuts!

'I'm not the only one who's crazy on this mountain,' he laughed. 'Will you marry me?'

'We'd better go down,' she said very pragmatically, 'before you get any more crazy ideas. Listen, I prayed you would come.'

'When the fire started?'

'A week ago,' she informed him very seriously. 'Right after you left! Where the devil have you been? C'mon, man, before Bea eat all the food, no?'

'You're sure you can go on? You're not frightened now?'

'I'm scared to death,' she admitted, 'but as long as you're here, I think I can give it a try. If you are——' For a moment she felt as if she should add another word or two. Something like 'my dear'. But her innate caution prohibited it.

'All right, now,' he cautioned. 'Remember, keep low, beneath the level of the smoke. There's nothing to worry about.'

She got up slowly, bent at the waist and knees. 'Why should I worry?' she replied with a little bravado. 'That's the man's part of the job. Are *you* worried?' Above their heads, far above, the mountain grumbled again, but the smoke and ash were already so thick that they could see nothing of what it portended. All Peggy had left to wear was the remnants of her skirt. When he jerked at it and whipped it off, she hesitated.

'I don't understand men,' she sighed. 'Certainly you don't want to—to—not here?'

'To keep the smoke out of your nose and mouth,' he said grimly. In a moment he had made her a suitable mask.

'You know something?' Jim Marston asked rhetorically as he headed his little safari down the mountain towards the beach. 'I'm not worried, I'm bloody well scared to death!'

# CHAPTER TEN

JIM MARSTON stood moodily at the bow of the highly polished Sea-Witch as they made their way into the harbour of Châteaubelair. Behind him on deckchairs Bea and Peggy Mitchell were sitting in the shade of an awning rigged over the boom. The diesel engines were turning over very slowly; Henry Coeurdeleon was at the wheel, his big smile gleaming, as if he had decades of experience dealing with a yacht of this size. Peggy got up, put on her big straw hat, and came forward to join Jim.

'Troubled, James?' He turned his head to look down at her, and offered a wry smile.

'It's been a long month since we came down off the mountain,' he commented. 'Are you *sure* you won't marry me?'

'Please——' She turned her head away. 'I—don't ask me now.'

Jim scanned the gleaming yacht. It *ought* to gleam, he thought. Every night this month I've gone to Fort Charlotte and asked her to marry me. Every night she's refused. Every night I've come back to the boat and polished and cleaned and slaved to work off my frustrations. And I *still* love her. 'As you wish,' he said, and turned his attention back to the harbour.

Her hand touched his wrist. 'Jim,' she said softly. 'It isn't that I—don't care for you.' He folded one of his hands over hers.

'You don't have to explain, Peggy. I've been some kind of a heel towards you. There, I admitted it, and it's not the sort of thing a man like me does.' A dry chuckle broke in his throat.

'It's not that,' she insisted, shaking his wrist to get his attention. He looked down at her. 'It's got nothing to do with you,' she continued softly. 'It has *everything* to do with me. I'm not crying crocodile tears because you seduced me. In fact, I seduced you. No. What bothers me, Jim, is that I am the worst judge of men in the whole wide world, and I—I'm so fearful of making a mistake.'

'Now that,' he sighed, 'I *don't* understand. But you needn't explain if you'd rather not.'

'I *have* to explain,' she whispered, 'for my own good, if nothing else. It's my father. I loved and honoured and respected him more than anything or anybody in the world, and he walked out on me—on us. I can't live that down, James. I just can't.'

He paused, unable to find an answer. The boat glided gently towards the pier, where a group of people waited for them. Her hand was still on his wrist, her eyes pleaded for understanding. Finally he forced himself to speak. 'I *still* don't understand, Peggy, but if that's how you feel, I'd not be the one to urge you otherwise. I have a few more things to do here in St Vincent. I love you now, dear, and I'll love you forever. If you change your mind, please—don't forget me.'

'I couldn't do that,' she returned mournfully. 'I wouldn't *want* to do that.'

He shook himself like a huge dog spraying water from his fur, and offered her a wintry smile. 'In that case then, love, let's put a good face on things. There are a great many people waiting for our appearance.'

When they stepped ashore, each with a smile, the little crowd led by Ada, Henry's wife, gave a cheer and hardly seemed to notice that the smiles were artificial. All except Bea, of course, who noticed everything.

Practically every member of the village was present, man, woman and child. Behind them four of the jitney-buses which served as taxis on the island's rough roads were waiting. Each bus was designed for twelve, could hold twenty at a pinch, and ordinarily did. There was a great deal of laughter, some raucous jokes, and a few pithy comments as the caravan pulled out of Châteaubelair and ran down the tracks that led eventually to the old village, and the path up to the Mitchell plantation.

Everything was almost as it had been, up at the farm. A month of rain and wind had restored the green to the soil. The fields were filled with almond saplings, stretched in long straight rows into the horizon, and already emitting the sweet smell of growth. Some of the flowerbeds around the house had survived. Peggy touched them lightly with the tip of her fingers. The house was gone, and the banyan tree that had stood beside it, but the foundations had been raked over, and green growth was nibbling at the outlines. Most of the truck farm crops had been destroyed, but within another month all the ruin would be conquered by the tropical foliage, and new crops could be planted.

'The land tests even more fertile than it did before the eruption,' Jim explained to Peggy as they walked arm in arm through the new orchards. When they came to the bluff where they had first met, they stopped. In the distance a group of animals was moving towards them.

'Why—it's Satan and Salome!' Peggy exclaimed. 'And Pepper too?'

'Ain't no volcano gonna kill no donkey,' Henry laughed. 'That ole man, he jus' went off at the first clap, he did. An' took the others with him. They gonna be all right.'

For the first time since they had come ashore, Peggy smiled a real smile. 'And now,' Jim announced, 'you'll notice we don't plan to rebuild the house in the same location. It's too dangerous up here, but at the same time the land is too valuable to be abandoned. So we're building the house somewhere else. That's our next stop.'

'You're taking an awful lot of decisions for the Mitchell family,' she said crossly. 'You may be wasting your money!'

'Never let it be said,' he laughed. 'And don't tell anyone else. Are you trying to ruin my reputation as an entrepreneur? Besides, I consulted at length with the only available male Mitchell.'

'You—what?' She tugged him to a stop, the fierce look in her eyes demanding an explanation.

'Yes, indeed,' he declared. 'I went over the entire affair with Andrew. He agreed completely.'

'James Marston!' She stamped her little foot, and only did damage to herself.

'James T. Marston, if you want to be all that formal about it,' he said, and laughed. 'They have telephones in Massachusetts, you know. Andrew and I have talked half a dozen times in the last month. By the way, he graduates tomorrow, and will be home next week.'

'I knew that, James T. Marston,' she said angrily. 'He's coming home, complete with a degree in agriculture. What does the T stand for?' The anger had turned to wistfulness by the time she reached that last question.

'I won't tell,' he chuckled. 'If you want to learn what it means, you'll have to meet me at the altar. By the way, did you know that your brother is getting married on Friday, and plans to bring his new wife home with him?'

'No,' she squeaked in surprise. 'I mean—no, I didn't know that. I had thought I would——'

'Be set up for life as his housekeeper?' he said pointedly. 'Well, it doesn't matter. Come on. Back to the buses. We not only moved the plantation house, but the whole village.'

Peggy followed after him, trying to hide her distress. Because he was absolutely right, of course. She *had* expected to give up the management of the plantation to her brother, and exist as his housekeeper. But now? Two women under the same roof? Troubled, she boarded the bus and watched from the window as Jim, using a portable loudspeaker, pointed out the bounds of the new village, about a mile from Châteaubelair. Cement and stone houses were already being built, to replace the cane shacks of the old place. And the new road went up the hill behind the village, two hundred feet or more, and there, overlooking the village and the bay, was the new Mitchell home.

'Not quite completed,' Jim whispered in her ear. 'But it will be finished by the time Andrew comes to carry his bride across the threshold. Like it?'

'Magnificent,' she sighed. But can it be home for me as well? she thought.

As the villagers and others from Châteaubelair gathered around, she did her best to look as if she were enjoying herself, but all the time her heart was empty. Until, an hour later, Henry came up to her towing a stranger behind him.

'Missy,' he said grandly. 'This here George Standish. Work for the Bureau of Forestry, he does. Got him something to tell you—very important!'

'Mr Standish,' she acknowledged. There was nothing this man could say that would be worse than she already knew. Or so she thought at the moment.

'Miss Mitchell.' The rangy black face smiled at her pleasantly. 'I hate to speak so,' he said. 'But I go to the old crater of Soufrière two days gone, you understand. Me and my crew, look to see how bad the fire damage. You know, very important. The rain forest the only thing to keep water in the soil. Without the trees, pretty soon we be like plenty other island—all beauty, no water.'

'Yes, I understand. Does this have something to do with me?'

'B'lieve so, lady,' he said, and seemed to fumble for words. 'You know, in the old crater we have for long time lake?' Peggy nodded. She had swum in the ice-cold crater lake a time or two before common sense overcame daring.

'The lake have gone down,' Standish continued. 'Maybe only half-way full from what was, you know.' He paused for a deep breath, and then rushed ahead. 'We find skeleton high and dry on new lake-shore, Miss Mitchell. Drowned man. The laboratory make the tests. You know, dental records. Fracture marks where leg is broken many years ago, huh? Today the laboratory say he you father.'

A wave of dizziness swept over Peggy Mitchell. Her hand fumbled for her forehead. The world became distant. A voice somewhere far away said, 'Quick. Brandy!' A pair of strong arms caught her, and the world went black.

The yacht was rocking gently in the afternoon swell as Peggy opened her eyes. She was stretched out in the cabin of *Sea-Witch*, on one of the two double berths. Jim Marston was sitting on a stool at her side, a worried look on his face as he chafed her wrists.

'My father,' she said, very clearly but slowly.

'Yes,' he agreed. 'No doubt about it. Your father. Not only a couple of physical identifications, but his watch, his wedding ring.'

'It means—' She had trouble with her throat and the words would not come.

'It means he's truly drowned and dead,' Marston said softly.

'No—no—' she muttered vaguely. 'That's not what I meant. It means he didn't desert me, Jim. He didn't run away. He *couldn't* come back. It doesn't matter why or how he fell into the lake. He *couldn't* come back. I wasn't wrong after all! He *did* love me. He did!'

As she tried to sit up his arms enveloped her and locked her tightly against his chest. Her brain began to percolate. 'I could use that brandy now,' she said, and when he had furnished it she downed the shot-glass of the liquid with one great gulp and coughed as the fire of it struck her belly.

'Of course he loved you,' Jim agreed. 'My father loved me, too. Now let me tell you something that breaks my heart, but ought to relieve your conscience, little lady.'

'Relieve my conscience? I haven't done—oh, lord, yes, I have. What?'

'First of all, I confess that my scheme to sell your arrowroot was strictly a scam, love. Harriman & Son was one of the companies that drove my father to the wall. I wanted a little vengeance—like sticking them with a tremendous crop of unsaleable arrowroot.'

'I—it's worse than I thought,' she sighed. 'It really was dishonest, wasn't it? I'll have to give all the money back. Darn you!'

'Well, no, you don't have to give anything back,' he said with a chuckle. 'I told you that in the trading business you win some and lose some. Well, the Harriman people found just what I thought of myself, a computer-paper manufacturer who wanted to run a sample using arrowroot as the starch filler in his paper. They sold the whole lot, Harriman did. And made a small profit in the doing!'

'I—I'm glad,' Peg said, very seriously. 'I would hate to go into a new phase of my life with that cloud hanging over my head. So they outsmarted us after all?'

'Fat chance,' he laughed. 'They got the arrowroot; I got the girl! Didn't I? Aren't you going to say something about that?'

'I—yes,' she agreed. 'I have some terrible problems that I must solve, Mr James T. Marston.' She ducked her head, hoping to hide the teasing gleam in her eyes. 'I can't live in my brother's house. You can see that.' He nodded. She looked at him searchingly. A tiny crease was playing at the corner of his mouth, but he only nodded again.

'And I can't leave Bea. She raised me, and I just couldn't——'

'Of course you couldn't,' he agreed. 'It would be silly to leave Bea behind.'

Peggy sat up on the berth and put her feet over the side. His arm slid gently around her as she leaned her head on his shoulder. He could feel the silken smoothness of her absurd red hair as it brushed against his cheek, and the world seemed suddenly ever so much better.

After a moment of silence she lifted her head. 'Jim,' she half whispered. 'If you were going to ask me the one most important question in the world, what would it be?'

'Well, now,' he teased. 'I have to think. It couldn't have anything to do with my making a fortune as your brother's backer in the almond business.' He shook his head while she dithered. 'And it couldn't have anything to do with the idea that I'd like Bea to come and be my housekeeper.'

'Darn you, Jim Marston,' she muttered.

'And it couldn't have anything to do with the fact that Bea is the best cook in the islands. So it *must* be——' He stood up, ducking under the low headway and pulling her up with him. 'How about this. Margarita Mitchell, would you marry me and *not* live in your brother's house?'

Two warm kisses later he put her down. 'You understand I'm only doing this because Andrew wouldn't want two women in his house on his honeymoon,' she insisted firmly.

'Oh, yes,' he murmured, and the little twitch had developed into a wide grin. 'But you wouldn't object to sharing my bed and board?'

And now they both were grinning. 'No,' she confessed, 'I wouldn't mind sharing your bed and board. Only I want to be married in the cathedral first!'

'Anywhere,' he promised. 'Standing on your head. Naked in the park. Anywhere. Let's go tell Bea!'

The companionway was too narrow for them to walk up side by side. She went up ahead. Somehow his hand rested on the sweet curve of her buttock as they climbed. 'Nice,' he commented, as they stepped out on deck.

'Exhibitionist,' she complained as she pushed his hand away. 'People are watching!'

Bea was sitting in the cockpit in front of a little folding table, her Tarot cards spread out before her. Peggy came round and looked at the cards over her shoulder.

'We have something to tell you, Bea,' Jim said.

The old lady looked up at him seriously. 'Sure,' she said. 'You two gonna get married.'

'How in the world did you——? We just decided that,' Peggy stammered as Jim, somehow seeming to understand, pulled her into the circle of his arms and kissed the end of her nose gently.

'Don't need no cards for to know that,' Bea continued. 'Obeah woman kin smell that in the air. You gonna get married in the cathedral.' Her wrinkled old finger tapped one of the cards in the pile. 'Only *that* you can't smell in no air, missy. Too bad you don't b'lieve in the cards!'

'And we need a housekeeper and nanny, Bea,' Jim announced with a straight face.

'Better b'lieve you do,' the old lady laughed. 'Cards say you gonna have six children!'

'Six children?' Peggy asked in astonishment as her fiancé picked her up and whirled her round.

'Six children,' Bea assured them, chortling. 'Maybe seven. The cards don't lie, but sometimes they don' count too accurate. Tell that fool man to put you down before he break your neck!'

Back on her own feet, Peggy, stretched up as high as she could on tiptoes and whispered in his ear. He laughed so hard he almost upset the little card-table.

'What she say?' Bea asked.

'She say,' Jim Marston said, dropping into the dialect, 'six children. Better you get this ship to go home, man. Lots of work, makin' six kids. We gotta start very soon!'

# Six exciting series for you every month... from Harlequin

### HARLEQUIN

## *Romance®*

### The series that started it all

Tender, captivating and heartwarming...
love stories that sweep you off to faraway places
and delight you with the magic of love.

◆

## *Harlequin Presents®*

### Powerful contemporary love stories...as individual as the women who read them

The No. 1 romance series...
exciting love stories for you, the woman of today...
a rare blend of passion and dramatic realism.

◆

## *Harlequin Superromance®*

### It's more than romance... it's Harlequin Superromance

A sophisticated, contemporary romance-fiction
series, providing you with a longer,
more involving read...a richer mix of complex plots,
realism and adventure.

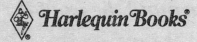

# *Harlequin Presents*

## is

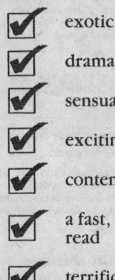

- ✓ exotic
- ✓ dramatic
- ✓ sensual
- ✓ exciting
- ✓ contemporary
- ✓ a fast, involving read
- ✓ terrific!!

*Harlequin Presents—*
*passionate romances*
*around the world!*